Who Knows Julie Gordon?

By Kage Booton

Who Knows Julie Gordon?

KAGE BOOTON

PUBLISHED FOR THE CRIME CLUB BY

DOUBLEDAY & COMPANY, INC.

GARDEN CITY, NEW YORK

1980

All of the characters in this book
are fictitious, and any resemblance
to actual persons, living or dead,
is purely coincidental.

ISBN: 0-385-15819-X
Library of Congress Catalog Card Number 79-8498
Copyright © 1980 by Kage Booton
All Rights Reserved
Printed in the United States of America
First Edition

For Hilda Karniol

Who Knows Julie Gordon?

The first time I saw Julie Gordon was at market in the local shopping plaza. Our carts almost collided at the far end of the second aisle in front of the meat counter that stretched across the rear. We backed and maneuvered, apologized with polite little smiles, then went our separate ways.

She reminded me of someone.

I saw her five or six times after that, a tall dark-haired, dark-eyed young woman, always in blue jeans, always an oversized bag slung over her shoulder. She obviously didn't remember our first encounter or even subsequent ones. My friendly good mornings were returned pleasantly enough, but always with faint surprise. And once when I came up behind her at the check-out counter she didn't turn although she must have seen me coming. That day she wore no make-up, I remember, and her long hair was pulled back in a high ponytail. There was a plain gold wedding band on her left hand. Another time, she was just pulling away in her late model cream-colored Lincoln Continental when I turned into the parking lot. I waved. I wave at everybody. She didn't notice.

Then a few weeks later, on a Saturday, there was Penny Wilde's pre-party get-together.

"Come over whenever the guys get back from golf,"

Penny said. We'd met in the parking lot at market. "The Brocks' bash doesn't start until eight, which means dinner much later. I told Joe none of that nineteenth hole stuff."

"The same word went out to Walt. I'll bring some munchies."

"No, don't, Ida. Mrs. Smith is coming, and you know how she prides herself." She hefted her grocery bag into the carrier of her bike. "And Mrs. Gordon might drop by."

"One of the new ones?"

"Fairly new, I guess. Quite pregnant. She'd been living in Alaska; her husband's still there, finishing up an assignment. Something to do with the pipeline. Mrs. Smith suggested I ask her."

"Thoughtful. No fun having a baby alone."

"She's not alone. She's got somebody at the house; a real oddball. He was trimming the hedge one day, and I stopped to say hello. He hardly spoke."

"Her father, maybe. Shy in a new neighborhood."

Penny shrugged her plump red-tanned shoulders. "He's nobody out of *Playboy*, but he's not her father, believe me." She mounted her bike. "See you tomorrow night."

The get-together had got together by the time we arrived. Because it was hot, they all were in the air-conditioned family room downstairs. Little old Mrs. Smith was whizzing around in her wheelchair, offering small trays of hors d'oeuvres she always brought for these occasions. The stereo was going. Penny and a dark-haired young woman in a sleeveless, long-skirted white dress were standing in front of the sliding doors.

"Ida—" Penny motioned me over.

Julie Gordon was the one I'd seen at market, and she indeed was "quite pregnant." Weeks ago, whenever I saw her, she'd been wearing jeans and crisp oversized white shirts. As she turned, the lowering sun hit her dark eyes sideways. They seemed for just one instant to bulge a little.

Then she was smiling. I remembered that I'd noticed her beautiful teeth at market that first day. She said, "I've met you somewhere before, Mrs. Pelham, haven't I?"

"The shopping plaza. We almost ran each other down."

"Oh, was that it? I thought longer ago. The Coast, perhaps."

"No, my husband's company is based here in the East. Someday, though, we hope to see Alaska."

"Alaska?" Brown eyes suddenly were watchful. "Why?"

Evidently she hadn't liked Alaska.

"Hey, Joe—" Penny moved away. I could hear her reminding her husband that his duties lay behind the bar, and not with Walt at the dart board.

I said to Julie: "Especially Prudhoe Bay. I'd like to see the pipeline, and what the companies have done about the caribou—"

"There aren't any Indians up there."

"I'm talking about the caribou crossings, the way the pipeline was dipped so they can step over, or raised so they can wriggle under. They can see their food and get at it, so they're not starving."

"Oh, yes, those."

She didn't know what I was talking about.

No husband in Alaska maybe? No husband anywhere?

"Have you always lived in Pennsylvania?" she asked abruptly.

"Off and on. Two of our children were born here. They're all away now."

"Married?"

"Ellen is. She's a photographer, has twin sons, and lives in New Jersey."

"Oh, dear."

"She doesn't mind. Our other two are farther away."

"You must miss them."

"Sometimes. We keep in touch."

"Your daughter, the photographer in New Jersey, what kind of work does she do?"

"Candid; people. What she's always done."

"She started young?"

I nodded. "I still have prints of shots she took when she was in her early teens, long before she began to sell. I've saved—"

Her face went strangely still, eyes curiously intent. I stopped, puzzled. Nobody could be that interested in somebody else's kids.

"I'm sorry," I said. "I talk too much about my—"

Penny came back. "Well"—she smiled up at the dark-haired young woman—"are you getting acquainted in the new neighborhood? Have you found things to do?"

Julie turned to her with a rueful smile. "If you want to call it that. My neighbors and I nod hello. And there's always that exciting break for grocery shopping." She ducked her head, long dark hair sliding over her shoulders. Then she tipped her head back. With thumbs and forefingers she guided her dark hair back into place. Her pale-polished nails were oval and curving. "To tell the truth, I haven't seen anybody I'd want to be acquainted with anyway."

"Oh, heck, we can fix that," Penny said. "There are plenty of gals your age around here, aren't there, Ida? Even a couple who are expecting about the same time you are."

"It doesn't matter." Julie shrugged. "I'm not the kind who enjoys sitting around having coffee with the girls anyway."

Penny glanced at me meaningfully. *She's hurt, poor thing.* "Julie," she said, "people don't pay calls on newcomers anymore. It's not that anyone is unfriendly—"

"I know all that. As I said, it doesn't matter."

"Maybe not. But why be lonely? Now why don't we, some afternoon, have a few of the—"

"No, Mrs. Wilde, please don't. I'm not lonely. And it won't be long now."

"Yes, well, if that's the way you want it," Penny said doubtfully. Penny herself wasn't a great one for staying home alone. She brightened. "There *are* things to do, you know. Block parties, auctions, strawberry festivals and the hobby shop at the plaza. You'll be surprised what you see there. They take things, beautiful things, on consignment."

"Speculation," Julie said.

"Consignment, they call it. I don't know. What's the difference?"

"That's a good question." Julie's rueful smile turned slowly to one of amusement. "Consignment. Isn't that a coincidence? That's the way I work too. On consignment." Some secret joke? Absently, she eyed Penny's plump pink arms and shoulders, the fuchsia gown with its spaghetti straps.

Mrs. Smith came wheeling up then. On one corner of the wide tray on her chair, was her daily allowance of whiskey and water. Spread over the rest of it were small blue plates of hors d'oeuvres. Penny and I each took a warm crabmeat cheese puff. Julie shook her head, smiling down at the white-haired woman. "I'd love to, but I'm on a special diet."

One of Penny's Meissen cups stood on a glass-topped table near the sliding door. Julie Gordon must have been drinking tea.

I helped Mrs. Smith turn her chair, and we started toward Margaret, Mrs. Smith's chauffeur-nurse-companion, reading a paperback in the far corner.

Mrs. Smith turned her head to look back up at me. "I'm surprised Julie Gordon is even here. It doesn't fit into her schedule."

"Probably she doesn't want to go to the Brocks' party alone. What schedule?"

"It's almost seven." Mrs. Smith lifted the heavy gold watch that hung on a chain around her finely lined neck. "It's time for her swim."

I leaned over the back of her wheelchair. "How do you know?"

"One of her neighbors. A Mrs. Wander; a goldmine of information. She says Julie Gordon swims religiously three times a day—morning, noon, and at seven every evening. Nighttime, she goes to work."

"What kind of work?"

"Nobody knows. But the light is on in that back bedroom upstairs until three or four o'clock in the morning."

"A writer?" Hadn't Julie said she worked on consignment? "Writers work all kinds of hours."

"If so, why doesn't she say? That's nothing to be ashamed of."

"Maybe she writes under different names." We stopped in front of Mrs. Smith's Margaret. "Some writers do that—one name for one kind of writing; another name for another kind."

"Porno?" Mrs. Smith at age eighty prided herself on keeping up on things. She shook her white head. "No. Mrs. Gordon doesn't look like the kind who would write porno. I think of her as more of—well, children's books."

I didn't. I looked over my shoulder, back at the two women talking, still standing in front of the sliding doors. Penny was absently scratching at the sunburn on one shoulder.

"Well, whatever she does," Mrs. Smith said, "she's not poor."

Oblivious to Al Hirt on the eight-track, and the rest of us, Mrs. Smith's Margaret was deep in romance, chewing gum, holding a tall glass so loosely that it tilted on the arm of the chair. It was empty except for bits of melting ice and a limp slice of lime.

"Time for a refill?" I asked. Then: "Margaret? Would you like another drink?"

Margaret surfaced. She looked at her empty glass. "Why, yes, dear. Thank you."

I took her glass and went over to the red vinyl-padded

bar. The men were shooting darts at the far end of it, and nibbling at Mrs. Smith's carefully prepared treats.

Al Hirt finished, and now Roberta Flack came on.

Joe was mixing Margaret's gin and tonic, keeping an eye on Walt at the dart board, when the phone rang. Not listening after he'd said hello, Joe slid the instrument across the bar, handed me the receiver. "Yes?" I said.

"What do you think you're doing?"

"What?"

"You get home here!"

"You have the wrong number," I said coldly.

"You heard what I—" Pause. "Julie?"

"No."

"I asked for Mrs. Gordon. Is she there?"

"Just a moment."

I took the phone on its long white curling cord over to Julie Gordon. She frowned. "Sure it's for me?"

"You're the only Julie here."

She took the white phone, turning her back to Penny and me. "Why did you call me here?" she said, low. Then, voice hardening: "We had to find out, didn't we? You want last-minute surprises?"

Penny was saying something to me, but I didn't know what.

"—nothing to worry about; I'm sure of it," Julie was saying. Then, angrily: "Okay, okay; five minutes."

She held the phone away for a moment, then put it back to her ear. Satisfied, she turned and handed it to me. I took it back to the bar, then delivered the gin and tonic to Mrs. Smith's Margaret.

At the bar again, I asked for a gin and tonic of my own. I glanced at my watch.

Sure enough, in exactly five minutes Julie Gordon said her thank-you to Penny, waved farewell to the rest of us, and started out.

I looked after her. Why did the tall dark-haired Julie remind me of someone? From where? When?

2

The Brock house was on the other, old side of town. It had been inherited by Mr. Brock from his father, who in turn had inherited it from his. It was set back from the road under ancient elms, painted slate-gray with white shutters, and dark wood doors with heavy, polished brass handles. The grounds sloped gently to the surrounding wrought-iron fence, and in the rear there was a walled-in garden where library teas and other charitable affairs traditionally took place.

"Wow, this is a biggie," Penny said as Walt pulled up in front of the open gate. The driveway was full, and couples were strolling back from their cars parked up and down the road. "They need a traffic cop."

"There's probably one around," Walt said. "I'll drop you ladies here. It'll be quite a walk back."

Penny and I got out. A woman in white, dark head bent, was hurrying through parked cars toward the top of the long driveway. Her back was toward us, but it looked like Julie Gordon. I wondered why she was going in the side entrance.

Holding up our long skirts, we joined others walking up across the shaded lawn.

"Whew," a man said. "I won't be long for this jacket."

"Keep it on a few minutes anyway," the woman said.

It was a surging sea of people, drifting to and from the living room, into the entrance hall, across to the dining room. The library door, as always, was closed. Someone was at the piano in the solarium. Probably Howie, the Brocks' only son. There was laughter, smoke, the clink of glasses.

Penny spotted one of the Brocks' married daughters and with a delighted wave started in that direction, pink shoulders and fuchsia gown a beacon in a sea of pastels.

"Ida, don't tell me you just got here!" Eleanor Brock was an angular, leather-tanned woman, with clipped gray hair. She was a golfer, and shot in the low eighties. "I thought you were coming early."

"I didn't say that," I reminded her good-naturedly. "You did."

"But what kept you?"

"We stopped off at Joe and Penny's."

Her mouth tightened. Then she gave an exasperated laugh. "Why is it that that young woman always has to plan something the same night I do?"

"It wasn't a party, Eleanor. Just Mrs. Smith and us. And Mrs. Gordon."

"Who?"

"Julie Gordon. Isn't she here?"

"She better not be."

Eleanor Brock did not tolerate uninvited guests or small children, even her own granddaughters, at her parties. I said, "I think she's a friend of Mrs. Smith."

"What did you say her name was?"

"Julie Gordon."

"I never heard of her."

She turned away to accept thanks and farewells from two departing couples.

I took a frosted glass from the tray offered by a gray-haired woman in a white apron, one of Eleanor Brock's ladies-by-the-day. Mr. Simpson, the high school principal, stopped to chat and, afterthought, asked dispiritedly if I had seen his wife. I had not. I talked with three members of the garden club, and waved to a cluster of Chamber of Commerce members.

Mrs. Smith's Margaret started to brush past me, a fresh drink in each hand. She lifted one high. "The old girl's two past her daily ration. This one is light, though. I made it myself."

"So who's watching? Margaret, is Julie Gordon here?"

"I haven't seen her, but we've been out in the garden. The old girl always holds court out there. It's easier with her wheelchair."

She went on her way chewing her gum, calling out, "Excuse me, excuse me." Margaret had a theory that chewing gum was the answer to a sagging chin line.

It was dusk now, and the ladies-by-the-day were switching on lamps and quietly announcing dinner as they passed. There were steamed clams and baked corn and chicken at the barbeque in the back garden; or if one preferred the dining room: thinly sliced roast beef, chilled salads, fresh fruit and cakes.

The party had thinned because of the heat and the delayed dinner hour, but still there were enough of us to make lines. The piano in the solarium was quiet.

Penny caught up with me over dessert. "Ida, will you scratch my back?"

"Certainly not."

"Who do I have to turn to? Joe's out at the barbeque with Walt and the rest of them." She looked at me pleadingly. "I'm going crazy. It itches awfully. Please—"

I put down my plate of angel food. "Let's find some privacy."

Out in the entrance hall, Howie Brock, the joy and bane of his parents' existence, was just cradling the phone. His look of annoyance suddenly was replaced by a sunny smile. "Powder room on your right, lovely ladies." He bowed, sweeping his hand.

Penny laughed as he mock-swaggered out.

Then she stopped laughing. Even in the dim light of fragrant flickering candles, I could see what trouble she was in. First, I rubbed hard with my fingertips.

"Scratch," Penny said grimly. "Scratch, scratch, scratch—"

I scratched. Part of her sun-dried skin collected under my nails. "You were destined to burn. Why don't you give up?"

"I always wanted a smooth glorious tan," Penny said wistfully. She dug into her party purse, and handed a small tube over her shoulder. "This helps for a while." She pushed the spaghetti straps off her shoulders.

I smoothed the pale cream over her plump back. It smelled like wintergreen.

Joe Wilde stuck his dark head around the corner into the hall. "Oh, here you are. Do you want some of those steamed clams, or don't you?"

"I want 'em, I want 'em—" Penny started away, pulling

the straps up over her shoulders, then turned, waving a hand. "Thanks, Ida."

"Okay." I went into the powder room to tidy my nails and wash the wintergreen cream off my hands. Penny had forgotten her purse. I picked it up, slipping the tube into it.

The living room was empty. Outside there were sounds of people laughing and calling out as they walked down the path through the side garden to their cars.

Then from somewhere nearby: "My God, are you crazy? What are you doing here?"

"The minute I saw you sneaking out dressed like this, I knew where I'd find you." A woman's voice, low, furious. "What do you think you're doing?"

"Attending to business, reminding a client by my presence of certain commitments—"

"You don't have to do that, you fool! Nobody's going to back out now! Everybody's getting what everybody wants!"

"—and making sure some stupid broad I know doesn't show and screw up the whole deal."

"You don't have to worry about me!"

"The hell I don't! The minute you get loose, we got trouble. God knows what you were up to this afternoon."

"Nothing! I explained why. Why can't you believe me?"

"After last time? Fat chance. You're getting greedy, babe; greedy, greedy, greedy— I can't trust you anymore. Now, you get out of here before—"

"This is the last time. I swear, so help me, when this is

over—" The words stopped abruptly. Then, a different voice, breathless: "You better get home—"

Outside, from the driveway, from the road, there came sounds of motors starting, cars pulling away.

But no other sounds now. I waited. Why had the argument in the next room ended so suddenly? What had ended it?

Was that a gasp I'd heard?

I hesitated, then started across the living room.

Whoever they were, wherever they were, they weren't in this spacious dimly lighted solarium. There was only a graying, bushy-haired man in a white coat collecting glasses and cocktail plates, stacking them on a cart of layered trays. The Steinway was closed and covered with its fringed paisley cloth.

"Who was just in here?" I asked him.

"I beg your pardon?"

"There were people in here talking just a moment ago. Where did they go?"

He straightened, looked around. "I'm quite alone, ma'am, and have been for the last fifteen minutes."

The three glass doors, the only panels of the hexagonal solarium not almost obliterated by lush hanging plants, were closed.

"I thought I heard—"

"The other guests have moved to the garden, ma'am."

I looked around uncertainly. This was an old house. Old houses have strange acoustics sometimes.

In the kitchen, the ladies-by-the-day were nibbling, scraping, stacking, and chattering. What was left of the party had moved to the back garden. Some of the Brocks' neighbors still were there, as were the Brocks' two daughters and their husbands.

Walt was handing a crème de menthe on crushed ice to Mrs. Smith's Margaret. "Where've you been?" he called out to me. "I haven't seen you since we got here."

I waved and looked around for Penny, her party purse still in my hand. Lights played along the stone walls of the garden, making shadows of the climbing roses, emphasizing the pristine whiteness of the Madonna lilies, and the rainbow hues of the old-fashioned flowers.

Penny, swirling the dregs of a drink, stood talking to the junior Brocks.

"Howie shouldn't have brought her tonight," Eleanor Brock said, coming up next to me. "She isn't complaining about the heat, but she suffers so visibly she might as well be."

"A basement game room is about as cool as anybody can get in weather like this."

"They won't be having their basement game room much longer," Eleanor said flatly. "They've sold their house."

Surprised, I looked over at her handsome son with his shining blond hair, and his fragile-looking, fair-haired wife. Another financial scrape? Was Howie gambling again?

"That house was our wedding present to them," Eleanor said. "At least they could have told us their plans. We had to hear it from Parker at the bank. Well, I suppose I shouldn't be angry, or even surprised. She never liked living this close to us anyway."

"Maybe they thought they'd be needing a bigger house now."

"What young couple needs more than three bedrooms these days? And anyway with her history, she probably won't make it this time either."

Eleanor Brock never had liked her daughter-in-law. On the other hand, she didn't always seem too fond of her own two daughters either.

Some of the neighbors were leaving now, and Eleanor walked to the side gate with them. I drifted over toward Walt and Mrs. Smith and Margaret.

The minute I saw you sneaking out dressed like this, I knew where I'd find you.

Everybody seemed to be dressed pretty much the same for this kind of weather. The men had shed their jackets. The women were in filmy cool-looking sheers. *Dressed like this?* Dressed like what?

We went through the house toward the front door. Passing the solarium, I glanced in. It still was dimly lighted, and the rolling table of trays still was there, but I didn't see the graying bushy-haired man.

On the way home, after we had dropped the Wildes off, I told Walt about the argument I'd overheard. "Whoever they were, they sounded as if they were coming to a parting of the ways. She said he didn't trust her, and he said she was greedy."

"Umm."

"You think I'm dramatizing again."

"Nope." We pulled in the driveway. "You left the light on in the den."

"No, I didn't. I haven't been in there today."

Walt stopped to let me out near the front door. "Well, it's on."

"I can see that." Walt always blamed me.

I had unlocked the front door and was reaching around for the light switch when I heard the sound from the rear of the house. A familiar sound, so familiar I almost missed it. I switched on another lamp in the living room and went directly to the kitchen to open the door down into the garage. I could hear Walt driving in.

"Somebody's been here," I said as he came up the stairs.

"What makes you think so?"

I waved a hand toward the back entrance. "I heard the screen door whooshing and clicking closed just as I came in."

"Wasn't the inside door locked?"

"You locked it yourself, just before we left."

"Thought so." He went to the back door, snapped on the outside light, and looked around. Leaving the light on, he said, "Leave this open in case you have to run."

He checked the main floor, then went upstairs. I could hear him moving around up there in his unhurried way, opening doors, closing them.

"Nothing's been touched, I can see," he said, back in the kitchen again. He clicked the lights and went down the stairs to the family room. "Nope," he called up. "We surprised whoever it was."

"Must have," I called back from the dining room. "At least the family silver is still intact."

In the den, we looked around. The desk was as I'd left it: unanswered mail, pencils and pens and a book of stamps in a blue crockery bowl, a stack of mail-order catalogs I'd been meaning to look at, and dust.

"What do we keep in the drawer there?"

"The usual." I pulled out the wide drawer of the desk. "Paper, envelopes, scissors—" The canceled checks and receipts nestled in one corner, rubber bands around them.

"Any money?"

"No."

Our chairs with the low table between were as we'd left them, last month's magazines and all.

Along one wall was a white-painted floor-to-ceiling bookcase. Walt had built it a month after we'd moved in. His engineering books were there, and his cherished tales of the sea. Mine were there too, everything from Poe and the Brontë sisters to the MacDonalds. And books on antiques and gardening, and photograph albums, and the encyclopedia our three children had used through their school years.

"There are spaces on those shelves." Walt glanced up as he headed for the windows on the far wall.

"There always are spaces on those shelves," I said. "I'm generous. I lend a lot."

"Tomorrow, I'll call Chief Henderson. Don't ask me what for."

"People are supposed to report prowlers. When the Chief spoke at Soroptimist Club, he said that."

Walt wasn't listening. "This screen is cut so neatly around the edge here, I wouldn't have seen it if I hadn't been looking for it."

I went over. It *was* a neat cut.

That was how they got in the first time.

3

The forecast was for rain, but the heat still was with us. Walt and Joe had an early morning golf game, so early I didn't hear Walt when he left.

Around nine, Mrs. Smith telephoned. She and Margaret had decided not to drive up to camp with Penny Wilde to see Penny's kids because Margaret minded the heat so. Wouldn't it be nice, though, if somebody could ride along to keep Penny company? I agreed that it would, and said I hoped they could find somebody.

After juice and a look at the Sunday papers, I drove over to the local service station to have the red gasoline can filled. It would be cooler this evening after the rain, and somebody in this house had to do something about that lawn out there. If one of us mowed, and one of us worked out in the garden for three-quarters of an hour, say, we'd get a good start on catching up.

I was reaching for the filled gasoline can in the trunk when Howie Brock pulled into the driveway.

"Hey, Ida, wait." He slid out of his car, or one of his cars; he had two or three. His golden hair glinted in the sun. "Here, let me help. That thing looks heavy." He swung it out. "Where do you want it?"

"Over there. Walt's side of the garage."

"Strategically placed, I see. The power of suggestion?"

I laughed. "Sometimes it works, and sometimes it doesn't."

He went back to close the trunk. "Want to leave the garage door open?"

"For now. We need the air in here. What can I do for you, Howie?"

"Got any good murders, ma'am?"

"Always." I turned, motioning, heading deeper into the garage and the stairs that led up into the kitchen. "I take it Linda's running out of reading material again."

"She's always running out of reading material." He followed me through the kitchen and across the hall to the den. "We drove up to her mother's place in the mountains last night after the party. It's so cool there we've decided to stay on for a few days, so we came back down to get a few things. But she's read everything her mother owns."

"There are some here—" We stood in front of the bookcase. I selected a Rendell, a Millar, and an early Ellery Queen. "So far as I know, she hasn't read any of these." I added the last book to the pile in his hands. "Enough, you think?"

"This will last her through today and tonight. Tomorrow afternoon the library up there should be open."

It occurred to me that Linda might have exhausted that library too. Not much suspense up there, she'd said once. I added a Stanley Ellin to Howie's pile. "I'm having coffee. Want some?"

To my surprise, he said he did. "I always want coffee. And Linda has to do a wash before she packs. You know her."

We settled at the kitchen table, the pile of books on one corner of it. I said, "Your mother said you've sold your house."

"She had more than that to say if I know her, and I do, so don't tell me."

"Not really. She just doesn't understand why."

He shrugged, spreading tanned spatulate fingers. "We want to move farther out, have some land around us. And I don't think it's a good plan anyway, a man having his wife and his mother living within a couple of blocks of each other, do you?"

"Depends."

"Not on the man, if you'll forgive my saying so. He's always the one caught in the middle. No offense intended. I know you're a mother-in-law yourself."

"No offense taken."

"We found an apartment in the new complex over on Reed Avenue; two bedrooms. No space to garden and that doesn't make Linda too happy, but it'll suit us fine until we find our place in the country."

"What will you do with all your furniture?"

"Store what we can't use. We wouldn't give any of it up, in case Ma asks. We know what belonged to whom in other generations. Mind if I smoke?"

"Not at all."

Howie always had been handsome. Even as a teenager, when I first knew him. No acne for him, no awkward gangly stage of development. Only the wavy blond hair, the guileless blue eyes.

I tipped my chair, reaching back for an ashtray on the cupboard counter behind me, and put it in front of him. I watched as he flared his slender cigar with a lighter of gold and bronze.

"When I was a kid," Howie said, "you didn't like me much, did you?"

"Same old Howie." I shook my head, smiling a little. "When you were a kid, Howie, I didn't think of you one way or another. I didn't see you that often. You were in military school."

"You heard my parents' side; you sympathized. That's natural. I was a trial to them; I realize that now. The cars, the girls, the bad grades."

"That was long time ago."

"I keep thinking about it lately. What would you and Walt have done if your kid ran off and got married at eighteen? To somebody six years older, working her way through college to be a psychologist. A waitress off campus, giving kindly advice along the way. But she wasn't a student, and she wasn't that kindly. Would you have done what my parents did?"

"No idea. I didn't know about that marriage of yours until it was over. What did your parents do?"

"Nothing."

"Probably what we would have done."

He stayed for a second cup of coffee, talking mostly about the past—when we all used to live in Plains, or Buffalo or Denver. Half the incidents or people he mentioned I didn't remember. But that didn't mean anything. My own children sometimes brought up things I'd have sworn never happened.

After Howie left with the pile of books, I retreated to the cool of the lower level. In a way, Howie had changed;

in a way he had not. In his very young years, he'd been so handsome he was almost pretty. He hated that, and I remember wondering at the time if that explained his sudden changes from moody petulance to sunny cheer. He'd outgrown that, or at least being obvious about it.

I finished the local paper, and turned to the Philadelphia one. It was a little after two when Walt came down the stairs. He was not in glowing spirits.

"How was the game?"

"So-so. Those damn little bugs were out, in our eyes, our ears, our hair—"

"Soon as the weather changes, they'll be gone. Did you call Chief Henderson?"

"I saw him at the club. We had lunch together."

"What did he say?"

"He asked if you found anything missing. Did you?"

"Nothing. Not even the liquor was touched."

"We scared them off. Probably kids."

Walt had reached for the sports section of the local paper when the front door chimes sounded. I went up. It was Joe. "There's nobody home at my house."

"Penny won't be late. Visiting hours at camp are over early on Sundays. Walt's downstairs."

"I hear you had a burglar."

"An intruder. Nothing was burgled."

"He might have been after that Meissen bowl on the pie table." Joe turned to the den. I followed him. Joe's rotund little mother had died as she wished, wearing a long skirt, high-heeled boots and jangling hoop earrings, right in the middle of her own antique shop in Hartford, Connecticut.

Joe's eyes swept the bookcase. "Maybe there's a rare book here, a collector's item."

"I'm sure not. Neither my mother nor Walt's has broken up her library. They both still have their own houses."

Joe went downstairs, and he and Walt started a dart game in the laundry room. I could hear the plunk, plunk, plunk against the board; their joshing. Then they moved back to the family room and switched on the baseball game. The refrigerator door opened, closed; opened, closed.

I mixed a crabmeat salad, and went out to the garden for red tomatoes fat enough to stuff. That's all the three of us had for Sunday night supper.

Joe went home before the eighth inning. Walt fell asleep during the ninth. I got up, turned the game off, went back to the papers, and fell asleep.

It was dark, indoors and out, when the phone rang. I groped for it on the corner table sectioning the two divans. "Hello?"

"Mrs. Pelham? Ida?"

"Yes?"

"Chief Henderson here. Sorry for calling so late."

"That's all right. What's up?"

"You knew Julie Gordon?"

"Yes, I know her."

"Could you identify her?"

"Of course. I saw her just yesterday—or, what time is it?"

"Almost three."

"In the morning?"

"In the morning. Monday morning."

I struggled to sit up, to wake up. My blouse was damp and clinging. "What's wrong?"

"There's been an accident."

"What kind of accident?"

He hesitated. "Auto. Her car went off the road on the ridge back of the golf course."

I waited.

"She's dead," he said.

I'd wake up in a minute.

"I know the car," the Chief was saying, "but I didn't know her, and there's nobody at her place. Could you come down to—"

Walt was stirring on the other divan, sitting up. He switched on the lamp. "Who's that?"

I handed him the phone and stood up, began to move around. Walt did most of the listening. Then: "Yeah, okay. Give us a few minutes. We'll be right there."

We changed out of our rumpled clothing. "Still no rain," I said as we drove to the hospital. The door to the morgue was around the side. A state police car was parked under a lamp post across the street. We went up the three brick steps. Chief Henderson was waiting.

"One of my men on patrol found her," he said. "About four hours ago. The kids go up there to drink beer, smoke, make out. Dark up there, isolated."

"Was she—had she been there long?"

"Don't know yet. Not too long, I'd say. The coroner was at the lake. He's on his way down."

Chief Henderson led us down the corridor and opened the door to a small, cool, brightly lighted room. It was tiled from floor to ceiling in pale yellow; the three other doors leading off it were closed.

Julie was all alone in that room, lying on a high narrow table, hands folded on the white sheet that covered her slim body to the armpits. She looked as if she were sleeping, napping in her white shirt. There were two brownish spots on the right lapel. Julie wouldn't have liked that. Untidy. She was wearing her wedding ring.

"Ida. Ida?"

"Yes."

"This *is* Julie Gordon?"

"Yes." Those long black lashes; the beautiful hands with curving nails so faithfully cared for. It was Julie Gordon all right. "Why is that there?"

I motioned. On Julie's right temple lay a white square of folded gauze. I could see one edge of a purplish bruise under it.

"Her car was smashed into a tree," Chief Henderson said, "above where the ravine is."

The rest of Julie's face was unmarked.

"Her car was forced off the road," Chief Henderson said. "Somebody shot her."

"I see. Well." I turned away. "I wondered why you were having her bandaged. You just covered it over."

We didn't talk much on the way home. And the house, when we got there, was quiet except for the bugs bouncing against the screens when we turned on the bedroom lights. We went down to the family room to sleep.

In the dark, hearing the crickets, we both were restless in our separate beds. I said, "There was something we didn't talk about when we were down there at the—that place."

"Yeah, I know."

"Julie wasn't pregnant anymore. Why didn't we talk about it?"

"I was just thinking the same thing."

Who could sleep? I sat up and switched on the lamp.

"Walt, what happened to the baby that was inside her Saturday afternoon?"

4

A few days ago, out of sheer boredom, the main topics of conversation in our part of town were the heat, golf scores, and who was having the next party. Now, on busy telephones, at market or the club, over coffee at the Sugar Bowl, the only subject was the murder of Julie Gordon. No doubt it was murder, everybody said. The door on the driver's side of Julie's car was hanging open, as if she'd tried to get out that way, then started to slide across the seat and got hit from there. Probably a .22, the butcher said at market. Could have been a .38, his young assistant said.

No gun had been found, no note. Any way you looked at it, it couldn't have been suicide, everybody said.

Local reporters, interviewing acquaintances and neighbors, learned they were just that: acquaintances and neighbors. Julie Gordon had lived in the area six months. No one knew her.

A real estate agent, triumphantly getting the name of his agency into print and on the air, allowed direct quotes: "She rolled into town in a Lincoln Continental, looked at three houses, chose one, and gave me a check that same afternoon. In full, drawn on a New York bank. She moved in a few days later. That's all I know."

"Was she alone?"

"I heard there was somebody living with her, but she was by herself any time I saw her."

"Sir? One more question. Where did she move from?"

"Beats me. I assumed New York because of the New York bank."

"There's furniture in the house. It must have been shipped from somewhere."

"I heard she bought it all brand new from a furniture store here in town."

That was confirmed the following day by the owner-manager of the furniture store, thereby getting *his* firm's name into print and on the air. The furniture had been paid for, upon assurance of immediate delivery, by a check drawn on the same bank in New York.

On the front page, along with the caption, there was a photo of Julie's car, its crumpled right front crushed against the sturdy trunk of a tree. The story continued on page three. Here, too, another picture: her open shoulder bag found on the ground nearby, a few feet down the ravine. A compact had spilled out, and a wallet. Or maybe it was a notebook; I couldn't tell.

It looked like the same shoulder bag Julie had carried whenever I saw her at market.

The feature writers did what they could with the little they had to go on. Who knows Julie Gordon? one asked dramatically. Where did she come from? What brought her here?

"Who is more to the point," Penny Wilde said. "There must be somebody around here who isn't talking. Pregnant and her husband so far away. Why would she choose this little town of all places? I don't think she even liked small towns."

"She didn't seem to think much of this one, did she?"

We were sitting at the kitchen table, having spicy bloody marys before lunch and looking at the newspapers Penny had brought with her. Hew newest pet kitten lay in a cardboard carton at her feet. She was trying to train it to ride in the basket of her bike. She looked up. "How come Chief Henderson asked you and Walt to identify her?"

"He didn't know what she looked like. He knew her car, that's all."

"Yes, but why you? You didn't know her any better than anybody else. My house is the only house she ever came to that we know of. You'd think he'd have called me."

"Maybe because he knows Walt. They get in nine holes before breakfast at least once a week."

"What has that to do with it?"

I didn't know. "You were away," I reminded her. "You went up to camp to see the kids."

"I was home before ten. It makes me so mad. I always miss the interesting stuff."

"Penny, believe me, it wasn't—"

"Well, I do miss stuff, dammit. I even missed when Jack Ruby shot Oswald on television."

I looked at her, shaking my head.

"I know it. I sound awful, don't I?" She leaned toward me. "Why do you suppose Julie came to my house when she never went to anybody else's? I thought it was because she wanted to go with us to the Brocks' party, but Mrs. Smith said she wasn't even invited."

I wondered how Mrs. Smith knew that. I said, "Maybe because Julie expected to see somebody at your house who didn't show. She didn't stay long, if you'll remember."

"Julie knew there'd be only you and Walt, and Mrs. Smith and Margaret. I told her at market."

We went back to our papers. "Hey, Ida, listen to this." Penny began to read: "There are indications that Mrs. Gordon recently had given birth. However, all doctors in the area disclaim any knowledge of Mrs. Gordon or the delivery of her child." She looked up, incredulous. "That's all. Those two sentences are the only reference to a baby, or even Julie's pregnancy, in the whole paper."

"They might be withholding information. Sometimes it's necessary."

"If they know the baby's safe, they could at least say that it's being cared for—"

They don't know where the baby is. We both thought it; neither said it.

"There's not much either about that man who lived with Julie," I said, "or visited her. Nobody knows who he is."

"And they still don't know where he is. That came over on the eleven o'clock news this morning."

When the front door bells chimed, Penny said, "Mrs. Smith and Margaret, I bet. I told them you promised cheese soufflé for lunch. They said they might drive over."

It wasn't Mrs. Smith and Margaret. It was Chief Henderson.

5

Chief Henderson was a tall, slim man, tanned, fair hair thinning; the same age, the same physical type as Walt.

"Do you have a few minutes, Ida? I'd like to talk with you."

"Sure, come in."

"Thanks, no. In the car. I want to show you something. I'll wait out here."

He started back to the car and I went in to change from shorts to slacks. Penny came running. "What's up? What does he want?"

"I don't know."

"What shall I do about the soufflé?"

"I haven't started it."

"There goes my elegant lunch. Okay, I'll go home and eat a baloney sandwich." She gulped what was left of her bloody mary. Then she picked up her kitten in its carton, and started down the steps to the garage and her bike parked in the driveway.

On the way to wherever we were going, Chief Henderson said: "After you identified Mrs. Gordon the other night, you said you had a feeling you knew her."

"I said she reminded me of someone."

"Have you thought about it since?"

"Walt and I talked about it. He said whenever, wherever we move, I'm always finding likenesses—physically, way of speech, mannerisms—to somebody we knew somewhere else."

"You've moved around a lot."

"Some. You're one of the first we met when we moved here eight years ago."

When I saw where the Chief was taking me, I pressed back in my seat. I didn't want to go in there again.

"I wouldn't ask this," Chief Henderson said, "if I didn't think you could help."

We went up the three brick steps.

A young white-coated attendant rolled her out. At first I didn't recognize Julie Gordon. No long black hair anymore, only a dark touch-up around the hairline. Eyelashes, blond and stubby. I had seen blond stubby eyelashes like that before.

They've washed the black mascara off her real lashes, I thought; she would have darkened her real lashes, to blend in color with the false ones.

"She didn't have brown eyes either," Chief Henderson said quietly. "They're blue. She was wearing contacts. Probably when you knew her, she wore glasses."

I nodded, not knowing how I knew. "Gold. Wire-rimmed."

"Blond hair?"

"Yes. Long." I gestured without looking toward Julie. "The same color, but brighter."

"When was this?"

"Years ago. It must have been New Jersey."

"All right, Fred," the Chief said to the young man. He took my arm. "Let's get out of here."

We went down the three brick steps into the stifling heat. Chief Henderson gestured toward the little shop across the street, with its selection of cookies and cakes and doughnuts in a glass case behind the shining window. The Sugar Bowl. "How about some iced coffee?"

"I don't think so, thanks."

"Whatever you say." On our way home, he said, "Where in New Jersey? What part?"

"Plains. That's near Clifton. And I didn't know her. I just saw her at the drugstore and places. She was a neighbor down the block."

We paused at a red light. Chief Henderson took off his hat and tossed it in the back seat. He mopped his forehead with a crumpled white handkerchief. "We can't get a make on her. No husband in Alaska so far. No fingerprints on file, no inscription inside the wedding ring; no letters or papers in the house. Nothing in her purse except make-up and a wallet, a phony driver's license, and an aspirin bottle almost empty."

"It wasn't a purse; it was a shoulder bag. The paper said it was found outside the car. Maybe somebody else dropped it there. Julie was inside, the right car door closed."

"The window was down. The purse could have been thrown on impact. There was seventy bucks in the wallet, mostly tens. No credit cards."

"No car registration?"

"In the dash. The car was purchased from a used-car lot in Harrisburg about a week before she turned up here."

"Cash?"

"A check on the same New York bank. Do you remember anything about the New Jersey husband at all?"

I shook my head. "If I ever saw him I don't remember."

We drove a couple blocks in silence, slowly, because of little kids with their wagons and tricycles.

I'd waited for him to bring it up, but he didn't, so I did. "What happened to the baby?"

Pause. "We don't know." Another pause. "According to the doc, it was a natural birth."

"Not Cesarean, then. Everybody's been talking about it, wondering. It's hardly been mentioned in the papers, or on the air. Did you look for the baby?"

His head snapped around. "Of course we looked for the baby," he said irritably. "We're still looking for the baby, out in the woods, down in the ravine. What in hell do you people think we've been doing?"

"How do we know if you don't tell us?" Then: "You just went past my street."

"I know. We have one more stop to make."

We turned down a tree-shaded street, passing Mrs. Smith in her wheelchair out on the lawn. She was supervising some of the neighbor kids playing croquet. That was how, much to her disgust, she'd broken her hip late last summer, stumbling over a wire wicket in the dusk one Sunday evening.

We stopped in front of a Cape Cod with a low hedge around it. I'd never been this far down this street before. "Whose house?"

Taking the keys out of the ignition, Chief Henderson turned his head, gray eyes level. "Julie Gordon used to live here."

He was watching me. "I didn't know where she lived," I said.

"You've never been here?"

"No."

"Has she ever been in your house?"

"No."

"Come on, let's go."

I needn't have gone. None of this seemed official to me, but I'd known him a long time, he and Walt were golfing buddies, and so, obediently, I climbed out of the car. A thin, dark-haired woman, coming around from the side yard to the front of the house next door, looked at us curiously.

The key he put in the lock had a white tag on it. The door swung open and then there was that waiting stillness of an empty house.

The living room could have been moved *in toto* from any furniture store window. There were no books, no magazines; no plants. Three lamps, but not one in reading position.

The dining room was the same. Not very good early American. The hutch held only six plates. "This room never has been used either," I said. "It wasn't meant to be. That fake centerpiece came right out of a display room."

"What is it?"

"A plastic bonsai plant."

"Whatever that is." Chief Henderson touched my elbow. "Out here."

The kitchen was the barest, most uninteresting kitchen I'd ever seen. No spice rack, no catch-all bowl, no cookbooks; not even a snippet of trailing ivy. Next to the toaster, there was a round container of salt and a tin marked black pepper.

"She was camping out," he said. "Look in the cupboards."

Because the house had an aura of being unloved, unlived in, I had no feeling of an intruder when I opened the cupboard doors. There were four white plastic plates, cups and saucers, cereal bowls, and glasses with worn-away buttercups on them. On the second shelf there were cooking pans and, upended in a far corner, an unskillfully hand-painted china plate with a pine tree on a hill, with cones on the ground beneath.

Below, in the cabinet under the sink, there was a box of soap flakes, scouring pads, and a roll of paper towels. Nothing else.

"No detergent," I said. "Evidently she didn't use the dishwasher."

"It came with the house. Maybe it didn't work. I understand she didn't inquire about any of the appliances."

The refrigerator held nothing but a carton of skim milk, an unopened loaf of whole-wheat bread, five brown eggs on a rack, a box of raisins, a jar of prenatal vitamins, and a yellow plastic bowl of oranges and apples. Maybe there was butter in the butterkeeper. I didn't look.

"As if nobody really lived here at all," I said.

"There are some signs." Chief Henderson was standing at the small divider between the kitchen and tiny back hall. With a well-sharpened pencil, he tapped the black phone resting there. "The number here is unlisted." He motioned me over. Next to the phone, there was the local directory with a white pad and a ballpoint pen (courtesy of the local furniture store) on top. "See this?" Now he was tapping the white pad with his pencil. He glanced at me, then began to shade over the top page of the pad, the pencil point turned sideways. Slowly the indentations on the pad became outlined. Not starkly, but they were there: Walter Pelham, 55 Chestnut.

I looked at him. "Walt doesn't even know her."

"That's the way your phone is listed. It means you too."

"That's why you brought me here. To show me this."

"Partly. The top sheets of this pad came out more clearly. We have those."

I didn't know. I went over to the back door and looked out the window. The pool took up most of the back yard. It was surrounded by a stockade fence taller than ours, six feet. There were no chairs, no tables. How could anyone have seen her swimming out here, I wondered, and then I saw the position of a rear upstairs window of the house next door. If a neighbor, the thin dark-haired one we'd seen just a few minutes ago, wanted to take the time and the trouble to stand at a certain angle at her back window—

"That's why Julie Gordon bought the house so fast," Chief Henderson said, "or that's the impression they got down at the real estate office. Because of the pool and the fence. For the privacy."

The beige carpeting on the stairs, I noticed as we went up them, had been well used in the years before Julie came.

"She didn't care," Chief Henderson said. "The previous

owner got transferred. Gordon didn't even try to dicker, the agent said."

The bedroom on the right was the master. There was a squat orange pottery lamp on the bureau. The glass-topped dressing table was bare.

"Underwear in one drawer of the bureau," Chief Henderson said. He flicked a finger toward the dressing table. "Cologne and powder and make-up in the top drawer of this one. And in here—" He opened the bathroom door. The cabinet over the pink wash basin was open. There was a yellow toothbrush in a glass, a tiny tube marked eyelash adhesive, toothpaste, and a jar of cold cream. There was a box of cleansing tissues on the tank of the pink toilet. Thin pink towels hung limply from the rack.

No investment of thought or care here either. I said, "What about the closet?"

"Go ahead. Look."

There was a pair of white sandals on the floor, and a blue weekend bag with a smaller matching case. On the shelf above were two wig stands; one empty, the other holding a shaggy gray wig.

"She never went anywhere," I said, "or that seems to be the consensus. Maybe some nights she just had to go out walking."

"We've had no reports of a tall gray-haired lady walking out late at night in this neighborhood, but it's a thought."

Hanging on the rack were two pairs of jeans, three crisp white shirts, and the white dress Julie had worn to Penny's get-together.

"All bought here in town," Chief Henderson said.

I looked over at the Hollywood bed with its tautly pulled white chenille spread. "Are her night clothes under the pillows?"

"They tell me the bed had been freshly changed."

"She must have used a robe and slippers. Even nude sleepers own those. What was she wearing when she was found up on the ridge?"

"Blue jeans, a white shirt, and black loafers."

"No underwear? No surgical pad?"

"Oh, yeah, there were those."

In the next bedroom, smaller, there was nothing. An amber ashtray had been emptied, at least it bore traces of ashes, but there was nothing in the wastebasket next to the small maple desk. The wastebasket had a brand-new look; it never had been used.

"No sheets on this bed," the Chief said, looking at the maple double bed, "and no towels in the bathroom across the hall." The bathroom was blue-tiled. "We found a tube of teeth stick-um on the floor in here."

"Her teeth were real," I said. "She'd have had no use for that."

"We know."

The room at the end of the hall was almost empty. A brown leatherette sofa, a long cocktail table with two back copies of *TV Guide* and a manicure tray, and a big-screen television console. The walls were beige; so were the tweedy draperies.

I looked around. "Is this all? Isn't there another room?"

"This is it." He was watching me again.

"Somebody said she had a studio back here."

"Who?"

"I don't remember. Her neighbors said she used to work all hours."

He didn't say anything.

I realized that we no longer were calling her by name. Now Julie was *she*. I said, "All she was doing so late night after night was watching television, doing her nails? Until three or four o'clock in the morning?"

"Looks like it."

"Mrs. Smith—yes, it *was* Mrs. Smith—thought she might be talented, gifted in some way. One of those who are very private people."

"Obviously she was private." He was steering me back down the hall.

"Julie worked on consignment," I said. "I heard her say that myself." Downstairs, I said, "We aren't here officially, are we?" When he spoke at Soroptimist Club, he'd said that most crimes are solved routinely, often by word of mouth. "Your police radio wasn't on—"

"I was going off duty."

"It's because of that imprint of my address on the pad next to the telephone, isn't it?"

"That, and the strong possibility you both might have lived in the same town at the same time. Hey, Ida, we're friends." His hand on my elbow, he guided me out the door. He turned, and locked it. "Right now, it looks like you could be my only lead."

The skinny, black-haired woman next door was sitting on her front steps, smoking a cigarette, and thumbing through a magazine.

6

In the first accounts of Julie Gordon's murder, the man who lived with her or visited her, whoever he was, was barely mentioned. The second day, the police publicly requested that the stranger make his identity known. He was described as a balding, dark-haired man, last seen by neighbors wearing dark gray work pants and a blue shirt. Any information given to the police by anyone who happened to be up on the ridge that night would be held in strictest confidence.

On the third day, the police reiterated their requests, promising anonymity to any witnesses on the ridge, and stressing that the man in the blue shirt was wanted only for any information he might be able to offer in the investigation.

"He's wanted for more than that," Penny said. "They're just printing it that way. Just like they're playing down the missing baby. The press cooperates with the police; don't think it doesn't."

"I disagree," Mrs. Smith said. "The only time the press cooperates with the authorities is in a kidnapping. The police don't release facts about suspects the way they used to because it might jeopardize the prosecution's case."

"There seems to be no husband," Eleanor Brock said.

"I'll wager this Julie had an abortion. That's where the baby went. Penny, here, tells me she was almost to term, and—"

Eleanor Brock never had stopped unannounced at my house in the fifteen years I'd known her. But I supposed seeing Penny, and Mrs. Smith and Margaret, and me, gathered around the ramp to Mrs. Smith's station wagon, talking so intently in the driveway would have been enough to stop anybody, the way the town was buzzing.

Eleanor Brock shrugged. "It could have resulted in serious trouble for someone. Perhaps what happened to this young woman didn't happen up there on the ridge at all." Then, as she turned back to her car, "Ida, dear, would you do me a favor? My neighbors are coming by for bridge this afternoon, and I need a fourth. Could you fill in?"

There were only two tables that afternoon. Summertimes, through the years, we played out in a tree-shaded corner of the walled garden with all its old-fashioned flowers. Sweet peas, snapdragons, hollyhocks. But not today; it was too hot. Today we played in the cool, dark-paneled library—ordinarily only the family's province. Here were the privately published, white-leather bound, gold-stamped volumes of memoirs and poetry; here the impressive family portraits hung. Four generations of the handsomest men who ever had lived, Eleanor Brock was fond of saying. The great-grandfather with his stern face and flowing blond beard, the grandfather with twinkling blue eyes and curling blond mustache, Howard Brock looking dignified—not the philanderer he was—with his graying blond wavy hair, and finally Howie: blond mustache, golden hair curling to his elfin ears. The Brock men.

"Well, I made it." One of Eleanor Brock's neighbors sighed contentedly as we seated ourselves opposite each other at table two. "Dear Eleanor didn't call me until noon, and I said, my dear, I'll never make it before three o'clock, but she said, my dear, two-thirty or else, and—" she chuckled comfortably, "here I am."

I leaned forward and added my tally to the other three on the corner of the table. "You didn't know about the game until noon?"

"None of us did. But you mustn't mind, dear. She hardly could have telephoned us all at once, could she?" Pale eyes were kindly behind shining bifocals. "Naturally, she called her older friends first."

It must have been about ten-thirty this morning when Eleanor Brock had asked me to "fill in."

Twice that afternoon, two of the gray-haired ladies-by-the-day came around carrying trays of iced tea and chilled cranberry juice and tea cookies.

"If you're working up to anything stronger, ladies," our hostess called out as we were changing tables, "just say the word. There are whiskey sours out there, and gin and tonics, for you, Ida, and some Chablis—"

"Not now, thanks."

"Too early for me, Eleanor, dear."

"I save my little nip for bedtime and Johnny Carson." Wicked laughter here.

At about four-thirty, I was dummy. I pushed back my chair, excusing myself.

"Can I get you something, Ida?" Eleanor Brock spoke automatically. We were opponents now, at the same table.

"I'm going out for that gin and tonic you suggested."

"Fine, but remember—" She was studying my cards laid up on the table, then looking back into her own hand. "The ladies aren't expert mixologists out there."

"I know. If the new man's busy, I'll do it. Can I bring you one?"

"No, I—" About to play, her hand paused in mid-air. "What new man?"

"The man who was helping with your party. I thought you'd taken on—"

She shook her head. "There were no men helping that night; only my ladies." In one smooth gesture she played her card and slid the trick across to her partner.

The ladies-by-the-day were preparing to leave. Glasses were stacked in the open dishwasher, and two mounds of tea cookies wrapped in plastic rested next to two well-worn handbags on the kitchen table. "Can we get you something?" one of the women asked.

"No, thank you. Tell me, who was that man working the party here a week ago Saturday?"

"Dear me, Mrs. Pelham, I don't know. I saw him, but—" She looked at her friend. "What did he tell you, Cora?"

"That he was here just to help with the cleaning up. He said it was a favor for Mrs. Brock and that he'd be leaving early because he had another job to go to."

"Do you know his name?"

Both women shook their heads. "Never saw him before," Cora said, "and I'm a native."

"It's not like it used to be, Cora. We used to know everybody. Times have changed."

I made my gin and tonic, and went back to the bridge table. My first partner of the afternoon won the prize, a mixed bouquet of summer flowers in a wicker basket. There were oohs and ahs and the usual post-mortems, but the talk didn't stay with cards very long.

"It sounds as if the police haven't made a bit of progress on the Gordon murder," my first partner said. Her pale eyes looked around worriedly through shining bifocals at all of us. "Who was she really?"

"Well, she must have been here for some reason. Could she have been the illegitimate offspring of someone we know bringing her troubles home to roost?"

"I never saw her, so I can't even know if she resembles anyone any of us knows."

That came from another of the widowed bridge players. Was that what they were pondering? Never mind she's dead. *Was she the product of all those times my husband was away on business? My* husband?

"And where did she get all that money?" someone else asked. "That house of hers didn't go for peanuts, let me tell you. I remember when it was built fifteen years ago, and it wasn't cheap then."

"She paid cash, it said in the paper."

"Same with the car."

"Somebody was footing the bill," Eleanor Brock said. "A relative, or somebody who's the father."

"But it needn't have been a he, Eleanor, dear. It could

have been a she who was doing the financing. I think women—wives and mothers—are even more sensitive to scandal."

"Blackmail, it's called." Eleanor, standing now, reached down to take a cigarette from the silver box on the end table. She bent her head to snap the lighter, diamonds glinting against her tanned hands. She looked around at us all. "I count myself out. I have no illegitimate daughters. My legitimate ones are enough for me."

Uneasy laughter.

Eleanor looked my way. "How about you, Ida? Julie Gordon was taller than you, but she had the same facial structure, and you're the only one here with those beautiful brown eyes."

"I don't have any illegitimate daughters either," I said.

"I remember how dark your hair used to be," Eleanor said.

I didn't know why she was saying what she was saying. Julie Gordon must have been in her early thirties. Certainly I hadn't produced a child at age eleven or so. What I said was: "I went gray because it's easier that way."

"Poet, and she doesn't know it." That was from my first partner of the afternoon.

Chuckles. Relieved chuckles all around.

As we were leaving, Eleanor Brock drew me aside. "Can you stay a few minutes, Ida?"

I hesitated. "It's almost dinner time. I don't even know what—"

"It's too hot to think about food. Let's have a drink, and talk a little."

Was this what the afternoon bridge game had been all about?

"Ida," Eleanor said carefully after we were seated on the sofa with freshened drinks, "according to the newspaper accounts you knew the Gordon woman when we all lived in Plains. How is it you knew her and I didn't?"

"She was a neighbor living down at the other end of the block."

"You lived on a cul-de-sac," Eleanor said.

"Yes, at one end. Then it straightened out the rest of the way into a street, don't you remember?"

She looked at me doubtfully. "It's been hinted in the papers that you knew much more than— You don't know something about—well, about anybody, that I don't know, do you? Company gossip, perhaps?"

I shook my head. I was sure I didn't know anything about her husband she didn't know, or at least suspect. "I'm sure Julie Gordon didn't have any connection with anybody in the company. I would have heard it somewhere, sometime."

She smiled. "From Penny, you mean."

I smiled back. "One of the many possibilities."

"Or the daughter-in-law." She meant her own daughter-in-law. "I understand she comes to see you."

"Rarely, and only on Sundays or late at night. When she runs out of things to read."

"You have good talks together?"

"About books, yes."

"So that's the attraction. It puzzled me." She touched my shoulder with a friendly hand. "Ida, I'm sorry about this afternoon. But you must admit, dear, there was a very strong resemblance between you and Julie Gordon."

I wondered how she'd be feeling when the truth hit the papers in a day or so, that Julie Gordon had not been a dark-eyed brunette.

"There are a lot of people with brown eyes walking around," I said.

When I got home, I looked at myself in the brightly lighted bathroom mirror.

Then I called my daughter in New Jersey.

7

Julie Gordon's name appeared less frequently in the papers now; it was being relegated to the back pages. No additional information was available to the press at this time, quote. All leads are being checked, quote. And if anyone had information, hearsay or no, about the man in the blue shirt, any communication would be kept confidential.

"Was he wearing a blue shirt when you saw him that day?" I asked Penny. "The day he was working on the hedge?"

"I don't remember. I guess so. Everybody who's seen him said he always wore a blue shirt. Not the same one, I hope."

"From what you said, I thought Julie Gordon was a neighbor of yours. She wasn't really. She lived on the street behind you, and two blocks down. Those are long blocks. What made you stop?"

She shrugged. "Mrs. Gordon was the mystery woman of the neighborhood. I thought maybe I'd meet her."

"Had you ever seen her before? I mean, when you lived somewhere else?"

"Somewhere else, where?"

"New Jersey, maybe?"

"No, why?"

"I just wondered if she reminded you of anyone."

"Nope. First time I ever saw her was at the shopping plaza right here."

It was almost two weeks now since I'd last seen Julie Gordon alive, and I wondered where she was resting. Still at that cold morgue in the hospital? Had one of those white-coated young men thought to put a soft warm blanket around her?

Didn't she have a mother or father who missed her? Or a concerned brother or sister who worried?

I began to buy newspapers from bigger cities, not only in Pennsylvania, but New Jersey, New York, and Maryland.

"What for?" Walt asked. "Don't you think the police aren't in constant touch with Missing Persons?"

"I know that. I'm looking for accounts of abandoned newborn babies. They found one in a trash barrel in Philadelphia last week, but it was black. A little boy."

"Why don't you play some golf? Or have the girls in for bridge?"

"In a day or two, maybe."

I saw Mrs. Smith and Margaret at market. Mrs. Smith, her lavender cologne wafting about, started by saying, "The man on the radio says rain today, Ida."

"I'll believe it, if and when. He's been saying that for a week now."

"Fortunately the heat doesn't bother me the way it does some people," Mrs. Smith said complacently. Then: "I heard you were at Julie Gordon's house with the police."

"Where'd you hear that?" There wasn't a good suspense story writer in that rack I hadn't read.

Mrs. Smith actually giggled. "Oh, a little bird."

"One of the neighbors, you mean."

"I'm not telling. What in the world were *you* doing there?"

"You got me." Chief Henderson hadn't asked me not to, but I hadn't told anyone but Walt about that visit. "Chief Henderson gave me a lift home and he had to stop off there."

"I wonder what for."

"Business, I suppose."

"No hanky-panky?"

I straightened to look at her, pretending shock. "Mrs. Smith!"

She laughed, delighted with herself. Then, sobering: "I shouldn't joke. Margaret and I have thought and thought. What was Mrs. Gordon doing up on the ridge alone in the middle of the night?"

"According to the papers, she was headed back this way. It was hot. Maybe she went for a drive."

"After just having a baby?"

"Nobody knows when she had the baby."

"Even so, at that hour. She never went anywhere; everybody knows that. Nights, she was always working." Mrs. Smith looked at me eagerly. "Have you heard what kind of thing she was into? Writing, or painting?"

I shook my head. "No."

"If I may interrupt." Margaret's auburn pompadour glinted almost orange in the morning sun. "I have a theory. It has occurred to me that Mrs. Gordon wasn't always working when her lights burned till the wee hours. It has occurred to me that she might not have been there at all. What if—" She leaned toward me over the five-pound sack of washed potatoes she cradled in her arms. I could smell her peppermint gum. "What if Mrs. Gordon waited until late every night, and then drove up on the ridge to meet somebody." She straightened, green eyes sparkling under mascaraed lashes at this romantic thought. "Some man."

"What man?" Mrs. Smith sounded exasperated. Obviously they'd been over this before. "Who?"

"Why, whoever it was she came here to be near of course. The one who bankrolled her. And the man she was living with, and he could have been her husband for all we know, could have found out about her secret love and followed her up on the ridge that dark night—"

I said, "She never could have driven away from the house night after night without some neighbor noticing."

"—and when he discovered the dreadful truth, that the child she was carrying—"

"There was only one car anybody knows about," I said. "He couldn't have followed her."

Margaret sighed, and put the sack of potatoes in Mrs. Smith's lap. They stopped at vegetables, and picked up onions and celery. Potato salad for them tonight, I thought.

Ever since I'd known Mrs. Smith, there had been Margaret. Who Margaret was, where she came from, I had no idea. But wasn't Mrs. Smith the one who had suggested Penny Wilde invite Julie Gordon to her get-together?

I was sure Penny had told me that.

The butcher. was chatty when I stopped at his counter for cold cuts. He leaned across the glass case on folded beefy arms. "Anything new on the Gordon murder?"

"Not that I know of. The local paper won't be out until late this afternoon."

"I thought you might know something, you and Chief Henderson being such close friends and all."

"It's my husband the Chief plays golf with," I said.

When I went out to the parking lot the sky was gray. The air was heavier, and I thought I heard a few rumbles. That doesn't mean anything, I told myself. I'd heard those rumbles before these past few days, and the rain had passed right around us. But as I was taking in the groceries, big splats of rain began to fall. Then heavier and heavier, coming straight down. It was hailing. I could see it, hear it on the roof. Strong breezes billowed the curtains, but I left the windows open, the air smelled so fresh and good.

Walt called to say that his late-afternoon golf game with Joe was off; count on him for dinner. That was okay. I forgot about my simple fare of assorted cold cuts and salad, and took a small ham from the freezer.

Except that by three o'clock that afternoon, the rain had stopped, the sun was blazing, and it was getting humid again.

"Hell of a thing," Walt said when he came home. "Penny took advantage of this, so Joe's on his way up to the kids' camp with her."

"They're Joe's kids too."

"Well, sure, but—"

"She's the one, every summer, all summer long, who

drives up to camp because he's always so busy working so late, ha, ha, playing golf."

"I always visited our kids."

"Sure you did. Twice a season maybe. If I could trick you into it, or the weather went bad."

"Now, look, Ida—"

"Okay, okay. I didn't like that crack about Penny taking advantage. I'm sorry." I was. "You want to go out to the club, right? I'll go with you. If you can't find a partner, I'll play along."

Sunshine and smiles. How a man's mood can change!

I went to my locker room; Walt went to his. We met in the pro's shop.

There weren't any of those under-ninety golfers sitting on the bench, so I teed off. One of my usual short, straight drives. Walt's drive was almost twice mine, but I'm used to it, and he's resigned to it. "You make it up on putting," he always said.

Only this time, the eighth hole, I didn't. Maybe it was because I glanced up at the ridge. *They found Julie Gordon somewhere up there.* The eighth hole is a tricky one, high, a small mountain. I overshot, and the ball went down the other side. That hadn't happened in the eight years we'd lived here. I'd always landed on the green.

Walt's chip shot was good. I went up the small mountain with him, and watched him sink a nine-foot putt. "I guess I'll just walk along."

"Ida, stop it. You'll get yourself out of this."

We stood up there, looking around for my ball.

"Probably it's off the course, down there in the ravine somewhere," I said gloomily.

"No, now, wait a minute, hon. At this angle, it should—"

We saw it at the same time. Blue. A patch of blue, darkened with wetness, but blue, under sumac struck down by the storm.

We went down the other side of the small mountain. It was farther back than it looked, that ravine at the base of the ridge. On the edge, when we first started in, I saw my ball. Not thinking, I picked it up and dropped it in my pocket.

He was lying face down, wet leaves stuck to his blue shirt. He was bald on the top back of his head. One arm was under him; one flung out. I didn't go very close. I thought of how fresh and clean the air had been during the storm only a few hours ago.

"He was shot," Walt said.

"Let's go," I said.

"Left side of his back," Walt said.

"I think we better leave," I said.

We climbed out of the ravine, holding on to each other, and detoured around the eighth hole's small mountain.

"I found my golf ball," I said.

"Good," Walt said.

"Our clubs are still back there," I said.

"I'll take care of them," Walt said. "You go in and change."

I stopped, turning to look up at him. "Shouldn't we notify—"

Walt nodded. "Right away. I'll call Henderson. Go on, now."

Eleanor Brock and the three women she usually golfed with on weekday afternoons were about to leave the locker room. They were dressed for play, and they'd had a few; quite a few. Arms around one another, they were singing as they left: "Eleanor has her grandson/ Eleanor has her grandson/ finally, finally, finally, finally/ Eleanor has her grandson-n-n—"

Well, that's nice, I thought. Howie Brock's wife made it this time.

Two well-tanned young matrons dressed in street clothes turned the corner from the back locker section. They shook their heads, smiling.

"What kind of game those ladies have would be interesting to watch," one said.

"If they make it to the first tee," the other one said, chuckling.

"I remember how my mother was when I told her I was pregnant that first time. Of course, the fourth time around she wasn't so—"

The door slammed on their laughter.

After I had showered and changed, I went to the pro's shop. There was a police car pulled off the drive directly out front, but no policemen in sight. No Walt, either. Our golf bags were leaning against the counter. The tall teenager who had been standing just outside the door watching Eleanor Brock's foursome tee off followed me in.

"Who brought our clubs down?" I asked him.

"One of the other guys. Chief Henderson asked him to." He racked our bags. "Mr. Pelham said if you wanted, I should drive you home and bring the car back. He said he didn't know how long he'd be."

"I'll wait awhile, thanks."

"He said you'd say that."

Two black cars and an ambulance passed the police car parked out front and continued along the golf course road.

"Want a Coke, Mrs. Pelham?"

"No, thank you."

He put a coin in the machine, and reached down for the bottle.

I wondered how they'd move the man in the blue shirt. He'd been there a long time. They'd have to bring him up from the ravine on a stretcher. Would he fall apart, like an overdone chicken?

I said, "I suppose you know what the police are doing out there."

"I know why they're there; I don't want to know what they're doing. I guess he's the other guy they've been looking for."

I nodded. "He was wearing a blue shirt."

"He must have been out there all the time. Chief Henderson said not to talk about it. He doesn't want people crowding around out there, trampling clues away like in *Helter Skelter*." He tilted his head and took a swig of his soda. "I haven't told anybody."

"Neither have I. How's your game these days?"

"Fair."

"Better than that, I bet. I've seen you out on the course with your dad every weekend since you were about eight or nine."

"I started before that."

Walt drove up then with a man in a black car. I went out.

"Come on, let's go," Walt said.

On the way home, I said, "What are the police doing?"

"Taking pictures. Measuring. Henderson hopes he can get some fingerprints."

"Do you think he can?"

"No idea. That's not my field. The guy had a wallet on him."

"What was in it?"

"I don't know. I didn't stay."

"I wouldn't have either. Julie was on the ridge, and he was down in the ravine. Same vicinity, so—"

"That's what Henderson thinks. He thinks the guy was shot at the same time, trying to run away."

8

In the summertime we had no immediate neighbors. The people on one side left with their children for a lake in the Poconos the day after school was out. The husband came home occasionally to check the house, but we rarely saw him. The elderly couple on the other side took off in their camper every July to visit offspring scattered around the country, and the widow across the street always left for Canada with her two black poodles on Memorial Day weekend.

There was nobody close by to ask whether or not anyone ever came near our house when we were away. Or entered it. I'd begun to have an uneasy feeling that someone had, and more than once. But I couldn't prove it to myself.

Then, the following Friday, I ran into the young neighbor next door. I was driving in as he came down the steps, heading for his car. It was noon, and he was carrying dresses on a hanger. "Parties up at the lake this weekend," he called out cheerily. "Thought I might as well get this done on my lunch hour."

"Good thinking. Have a wonderful time."

"Always do. Hey—" He detoured. A thin, balding man in his thirties, he cut across the grass between our driveways as I started for my own front door. "We've been following the Julie Gordon thing. My wife says she saw her a couple of times driving down this street. She says the car always slowed down in front of your house."

"A Lincoln Continental?"

"That's what she said. Cream-colored."

"Is your wife certain a woman was driving?"

"If that's what she said, she's certain; take it from me. She checks things. She said she was relieved that the car crawled past your house instead of ours." The lobes of his longish ears turned pink. "Sometimes my wife has unwarranted suspicions. I never even saw Mrs. Gordon. And my secretary must be as old as you are."

"I see. So your wife thought whoever drove by was hoping for a glimpse of my husband, or me, or your wife, or you?"

"Not us, no! You or your husband!"

"You should report this to Chief Henderson, you know."

"We can't do that. My wife said I should tell you on the chance you or your husband—" His ears grew pinker. "We don't want to be involved."

"I understand. Thank you. Have a good weekend."

He was bending into his car, carefully hanging up the dresses on the side hook, as I went into the house.

The mail hadn't yet come; there was nothing new to read. I made lemonade, and had chilled consommé for lunch.

Penny Wilde biked over to collect for a baby present. Another new one on the next block had arrived during the night. A girl.

"How many others are we expecting?" I asked as I dug into my handbag.

"No more due until September," Penny said cheerfully. She loved it when other people had babies. "Here. I brought you some newspapers I picked up this morning. Something about a Harlon Pierce. Nothing much else in them though."

There wasn't. An undisclosed source told a local reporter that there had been identification on the body of the man in the blue shirt, and that it was being checked. Harlon Pierce, the name was.

What good was that? Probably whatever the wallet contained was no better than Julie Gordon's driver's license had been.

I called Chief Henderson to tell him about my neighbor. "He said his wife saw Julie driving past our house. Slowly. Two times."

"More times than that. I heard about it."

"How?"

"You have other neighbors. Farther down the street, but they are there. Anything else?"

"Just something I thought of."

"Shoot."

"That Saturday when we stopped at Penny Wilde's before the Brock party, I tried to strike up a conversation with Julie Gordon about Alaska. I don't think she knew what I was talking about."

"How so?"

"If her husband is working up there on the pipeline, wouldn't the words Prudhoe Bay have been familiar to her? Wouldn't she have known about the buildings on stilts, and the crossings built for the caribou herds?"

"Seems so. Anything else?"

"No. I'm wasting your time. I don't know why I even telephoned."

"You're not wasting my time. Any thought or recollection you have, I want you to call me, okay?"

"Okay." I started to hang up.

"Ida?"

"Yes?"

"We aren't getting anywhere in Plains. That street, that circle you used to live on? All new people."

"That's the way it was when we were there. Company transfers. When we left after three years, there were only two families who had been there when we came."

"We don't even have a name to go on," he said. "And only a vague physical description."

And I wasn't absolutely certain it was New Jersey. Could I be remembering Julie Gordon, the way she used to be, from Buffalo? Denver? "I wish I could be more help," I said.

"You're not the only one," Chief Henderson said.

We hung up.

Then, and I don't know why I did it, but I did. Possibly because there was nothing new to read in the house. I went to see the thin, dark-haired neighbor of Julie Gordon.

The name on the mailbox was Wander. "I'm Ida Pelham," I said.

"I know who you are. A relative of the Brock family."

"No relation. May I come in, Mrs. Wander?"

"You sure can." She was wearing Kelly green party pants and a sleeveless overblouse. A cigarette in one hand, a magazine under her arm, she opened the door wide. "This is great. I've had more company since my neighbor was killed than all the time we've lived in this neighborhood. Have a seat." She waved her arm, dropping ashes on the scarlet carpeting. "Everybody thinks you're connected with the Brocks on account of your husband's big job, and you moving here when they did."

"The only connection is business." I sat down on a sofa upholstered in gray, splashed with red cabbage roses. "When Mr. Brock was transferred back here to the home office, my husband and Joe Wilde were transferred with him. The Brocks and the Wildes were delighted. This is their home town."

"I know. Doesn't everybody? How about you?"

"We're used to changing locations."

"Smart." She looked at me admiringly. "Pays off to stick with the boss, don't it? So Brock inherits all this money, retires, and your old man moves up and in."

"Mr. Brock decided years ago to retire at sixty-two." The truth. "Tell me, Mrs. Wander—"

"Naomi May." She dropped into the red-flowered chair opposite me, deposited her magazine (*Confession*) on the floor at her feet, and turned to the side table to tamp out her cigarette in a souvenir ashtray from Atlantic City. "My name is Naomi May."

"Naomi May; yes. Naomi May, you must be the neighbor who told Mrs. Smith about Julie Gordon's habits. About when she swam, about the light burning through the night in the back of the house—"

"Yeah, it was me." She nodded complacently. Evidently she'd been asked this question before. "I ran into the old girl grocery shopping one day, her and that red-dyed babysitter of hers, and I just happened to mention I lived next door to the new lady in town. All of a sudden the old girl was real friendly."

I nodded. "Mrs. Smith is always friendly."

"I don't know about that. One time when I was grocery shopping, and I was talking to her and her babysitter, Mrs. Wilde came up to talk about a party or something, and the old girl said Mrs. Wilde ought to invite my neighbor too on account of she didn't know anybody in town. My neighbor was way across the store, and I was standing right there, but she didn't mention me. I don't know anybody in my neighborhood either." Thin mouth turned down, Naomi May reached for another cigarette. "The only reason they were friendly to me was their nosiness."

Not downright nosiness; not quite that word. But that could explain Mrs. Smith's suggestion that Penny Wilde include Julie in the get-together. I said, "Sometimes older people take more interest in other people's lives because there's not much going on in their own."

"Well, I'm a lot younger than she is, and I haven't got anything great going for me either."

"Yes, but you can get out and around. What about the man in the blue shirt? Did you know him? The one next door?"

That perked Naomi May up a little. "He lived there. Don't believe what they say in the papers."

"I don't. You're the one who would know."

She nodded, pleased. "Well, he was around the yard a

lot, or fussing over the car. He had the hots for that car, you better believe. Sometimes at night, late, I'd hear him taking it out."

"Are you sure it was he? Maybe she—"

Naomi May shook her head. "He never took it out days. That's when she used it. Days he took the bus. I used to see him waiting down on the corner. No, it was him all right. I sit here alone in the dark most nights, waiting for my old man to roll in. You probably heard. We don't get along so hot."

"No, nobody told me. I'm sorry to hear it."

"Me too. I'm a pretty good cook, I keep a clean house, and I'm no cold fish in bed, but—" She lifted thin shoulders.

"If you heard the car going out, and it was late and dark, how could you be sure a man was driving?"

"The street light, and I'd be watching. I'd hear the garage door go up. They never left the car in the driveway; they always put it away. They had one of those automatic door openers."

"Did he stay out long? Did you see or hear him come back?"

"Sometimes. Sometimes he'd be gone like around an hour, sometimes he'd be gone most of the night. He was all dressed up."

"How do you know, if he was always in the car?"

"Well, once he was anyway. Once at the end of the driveway he got out to check a front tire. He had on a real sharp sport jacket. He didn't look bad at all."

"But you never saw those two go anywhere together?"

She shook her head. "Just that last time."

"When was that?"

"That Sunday morning. It wasn't light out yet. My old man was home, but I got up again. He'd had more'n his share, and no shower after work. You know how it is."

I nodded. I read Ann Landers and Dear Abby, too. "What time did your husband get home?"

"It was after two. Early for him. He boozes, but he's got a good construction job. That's how come we got this nice big house here. I couldn't make him eat anything, and he wouldn't take a shower—"

"You told me," I said quickly. "So your neighbors drove out about—about when?"

"Four-thirty, maybe. Later, maybe. Like I said, it was still dark out but the sky was beginning to get light."

"And you're certain there were two of them?"

"Oh, sure. They had a lot of junk in the back seat."

"What kind of junk?"

"Boxes, barrels; I don't know. She was sitting sort of slumped in her seat, her head against the window. Looked like she had a pillow." Naomi May leaned forward. "Say, how'd you like a nice cold beer?"

."Sounds good, but I can't. I still have marketing to do."

"So what? Just don't stand close to anybody, and don't breathe out fumes. I got plenty out there." She stood up. "Come on, one won't hurt you."

"Okay, let's split one." Then, as she started for the kitchen: "Did you talk with your neighbors much?"

"No way," she said over her shoulder. "When they first moved in, I really flipped, you know? I had a picture, her asking me over, us being about the same age, you know, and that we'd be lolling around her pool, yakking together, her old man away, and mine too, in a manner of speaking—" I didn't hear the rest of it.

The refrigerator door slammed, and then she was back with two frosted brown bottles, a glass upended over the neck of each.

"They weren't friendly," Naomi May said. "You were lucky to get a hello out of them. I stopped trying. You don't have to hit me over the head. At night, right after she got her phone call, she'd go upstairs and close the drapes. As if I cared what she was doing in that back room."

"You noticed she pulled the draperies, just the same. What do you mean, after she got her phone call?"

"Summers, windows open, you hear everybody's phone around here. She used to get a call around nine every night. Then her light would go on upstairs."

"Do you think that was a signal of some kind?"

"What for?"

"No idea. Maybe she had an answering service, and that's when the service called in."

"What would she need one for? She didn't work, not even around the house. The guy did most of it; even took the garbage out. She wasn't much of a cook either."

I laughed. "Now, how do you know that?"

"Easy. Never any good smells from that house; not even spaghetti sauce on Saturday night, or roast chicken on Sunday."

"They kept their windows closed." Just then, I remembered. Hot weather, but all the windows in Julie Gordon's house had been closed. No. Wrong. The police would have closed those windows, and sealed them. But what else did I remember? "Did they get along? Julie and that man in the blue shirt?"

"He was there, wasn't he?"

"That doesn't mean anything. You must have seen them together. Surely you could tell. Was he a relative, or a lover, or what?"

"Don't ask me. The only times I ever saw them together was when he came out by the pool. She called him Benny; I heard that. He'd say something, she sat up, he'd hold out his hands, she grabbed, and he'd get her on her feet. He was very careful of her."

"What an odd way to put it, Naomi May. Not loving, not kind; just careful."

"That's the way it looked to me."

"She never really swam?"

"Oh, yeah, she swam. And good too. Australian crawl, my old man said. He was a lifeguard in high school. The last day I saw her, she was laying there on the deck, her belly up to the sun. Like always, after a swim. She had a pink wash cloth over her face. She didn't want the sun anywhere but on her belly, I figured. For the baby in there, you know?"

"Yes." I said, "You talked about having more company than usual lately."

"Not friendly and nice like you, though. Just police and reporters."

"Police and reporters can be friendly. What police? Chief Henderson?"

"Him and another one. They said not to talk too freely to the reporters. They said if certain things appeared in print, it might impede the investigation. Exact words.

One lady reporter didn't like it much when I told her
that."

"I believe it." I thought about the name Pelham on a
white pad in Julie Gordon's kitchen, indented there I supposed when she was looking for my address. There were
no other marks as I remembered; none I saw. "Did you
tell the police about Julie's nine-o'clock phone calls?"

"I'll say. I know better than not to cooperate with the
police. Say, you're not an undercover reporter, are you?
Chief Henderson wouldn't like it if I—"

"No." I put down my glass. "No, I'm not. Thank you
for your hospitality, Naomi May."

"You haven't finished your beer."

"I know. We'll get together again soon."

She followed me to the door. "I hope so, now that
we're acquainted."

As I was getting into my car, the mailman pulled up in
front of Julie Gordon's house. He leaned out and put a
long white envelope into Julie Gordon's mailbox.

9

Chief Henderson had said, and just a couple of hours ago: "Any thought or recollection you have, call me, okay?" And at that Soroptimist Club dinner meeting last fall, he'd said, "Most of our leads come from people we talk to."

But he also had said, at that same dinner meeting: "And then we have the would-be informants. The vindictive ones who have personal axes to grind; those who claim to have seen something they couldn't have seen; those who claim knowledge they can't possibly possess, and those with vivid imaginations who simply want to get into the act. Their names and pictures appear in the newspapers, on the television screens. Publicity can be pretty heady stuff. But we check into every bit of information we can get, even hearsay; we can't afford not to. Ninety percent of the time, it's worthless. It's the other ten percent, the bits and pieces, that can add up."

Vivid imagination. How often had I heard those words in my own house.

Certainly the police were checking Julie Gordon's mail. Probably that white envelope just delivered to her mailbox was addressed to Occupant anyway.

I decided not to call Chief Henderson again this day.

Penny, round face as pink as the shorts she was wearing, biked up as I pulled in the drive. "How did you make out for the new baby?" I asked.

"Only fourteen bucks. What can we buy for that these days? Nobody's generous anymore."

"Everybody's still recovering from June bridal showers and neighborhood wedding presents. Want some lemonade?"

"You betcha!". She parked her bike, and we went in through the garage. "You haven't asked about my kitten."

"Oh, your kitten. Where is she?"

"Home. She doesn't like the bike anymore."

"You should have learned from your other experiences, Penny. Kittens aren't like puppies."

We carried our frosted lemonades down to the cool of the family room.

"Wasn't it eerie," Penny said, "seeing that picture of the man in the blue shirt in last night's newspapers? He didn't look exactly alive, I've seen police pictures of live ones worse than that, but knowing he was dead when it was taken—" She hunched plump shoulders. "He had blue eyes and false teeth, the paper said."

"You saw him when he was alive."

"Only once, close up—the time he was trimming the hedge. The neighbors on either side identified him, or at least verified that he was the guy they'd seen next door. They could have called me."

Naomi May had not mentioned that she had helped with the identification. I said, "What did he look like?"

"You saw him. Oh." Peggy stopped. "You didn't really, did you? When you saw him, he was on his stomach, dead."

The phone rang. "I'll go up and get the pitcher," Penny said.

It was Ellen. "I found several possibles, Mother. Sorry I took so long. The darn things are stashed away all over the house."

"Any dates?"

"Some. The ones you might be interested in were taken when I was in high school."

"That would make it New Jersey, wouldn't it?"

"Yes. Want me to put them in the mail?"

"Not this minute. I'll call you back tonight. How are the kids?"

"Terrible twos, remember? Why don't you ask how *I* am?" A little more talk, and we hung up.

"Your daughter in New Jersey?" Penny came down the stairs, pink on pink, carrying the pitcher of lemonade with its jingling ice cubes.

"Yes. Ellen. You started to tell me about the man in the blue shirt. Harlon Pierce, it said in the paper."

"Well, maybe. He didn't look like a Harlon Pierce to me."

"What *did* he look like?"

"Not very big; maybe five-six or seven. Black hair, thinning on top; the wisps shiny and slicked back. Tanned on top of his head; his hands too. I noticed when he was trimming the hedge. His nails were clean, clipped short. Not like the Brocks' gardener. That one always looks like he needs a bath."

I'd never been that close to the Brocks' gardener. "Has anyone done anything about a present for the Brocks' new baby?"

"Not that I know of. Nobody's even seen it; not even Mrs. Brock. It's still at the lake with Linda and her mother. In an incubator, I hear."

"Why an incubator?"

"Merely a precaution, Mrs. Brock said. She suspects they didn't make it to the hospital up there, not that Howie would admit it. Baby Howard should have been born right here where he belongs, she said. She hates it that they're there. She said Linda's mother is an awful housekeeper; they have mice."

"Penny, anybody living in the middle of the woods has an occasional field mouse or two."

"I'm just telling you what she said. She said Linda's mother reads in bed, and eats crackers and cheese. That's bound to draw mice, she said." Penny frowned. "I don't know what that would have to do with an incubator, though, do you?"

"Could be it's only a story, Howie's way of keeping the two new grandmothers apart. He dislikes unpleasantness."

"He dislikes it! How about Linda? Mrs. Brock tried to break up that marriage right from the beginning, just as she did Howie's first one."

Howie had said once that his parents had done nothing about his first brief marriage, and all I knew about the second one was that Eleanor Brock never spoke of Linda by name. It was always "*the* daughter-in-law."

"They don't get along," Penny said. "One day after we'd moved back here—" She paused for a deep swallow of her lemonade. "I was working on the hospital drive that year and when I got to Linda's, Mrs. Brock was just leaving. She looked grim. Linda was in tears. Seems Mrs. Brock had caught her working out in the garden with no gloves."

"They argued over that?"

Penny nodded. "Linda was wearing her rings while weeding. That big diamond on her left hand is a Brock heirloom."

"Oh-oh."

"You said it. Well, Howie and Linda are still together. Howie may have his faults but he's not like his father. He doesn't play around. He's been straight with Linda." She put her glass down and stood up. "And Linda has her baby now. The only Brock male in the current generation. Nobody can take that away from her."

After Penny left, I called Walt at the office.

"Why you? Why don't you just tell Henderson?"

"Because I think my way is better," I said. "And that isn't what I asked you."

"Right you are."

"It'll be for only a day or two."

"Okay, sure. Go ahead. I just hope you know what you're doing, that's all."

10

The drive from our house to the Harrisburg airport took forty-five minutes; the flight to Newark forty-five more.

Ellen met me at the carousel in Terminal 2. Since the advent of the twins, it was the only way. She held each firmly by the hand as we kissed hello. "Want them, or carry your own bag?"

I opted for the flight bag.

We went down to the lowest level, to parking. Sounds of ringing heels, voices, cars starting and stopping, doors slamming; an enormous echo chamber of concrete and ceramic tile. "My memory of my high school years would be better than yours, Mother."

"I'm counting on it."

We shared the twins; one on the back seat with me, one up front with Ellen. Likable little guys, towheads, chatterboxes.

After they were fed and bathed, and talked with their father, who was on business in Detroit, Ellen and I went down to the darkroom in the basement. "I enlarged some of them." Ellen slid the bolt high on the door and reached in to pull the string attached to the chain on the overhead light bulb. "But there's one—" She unclipped the five-by-sevens hanging on the drying rack. "Here, see what you think."

All were of young women. One wearing cut-off blue jeans was smiling into the camera, her baby papooselike on her back. Another showed two young mothers lying on a blanket in swimsuits, plumply diapered offspring peering through the mesh walls of a playpen close by on the grass. Still another was the photo of a small child and a puppy. Ellen pointed wordlessly. In the background, in the yard next door, there was a woman sunning on a redwood chaise longue. Her brief halter-top dress was yellow. Pale hair swept away from a face upturned to the sun; eyes were closed behind glasses low on a tilted nose. Her child's arrival was not far in the future.

"I have others that must have been taken the same day," Ellen said, "but this is the clearest."

I studied the print.

All in profile, but I'd seen that face before. And recently. The long indolent lines of the body weren't unfamiliar either. "Younger," I said, "but I'd swear she's the same one."

"It seemed the closest from what you told me on the phone. Better look at the rest of them."

I looked at the rest of them, then went back to the blond young woman so obviously pregnant on the chaise longue.

"She lived next door to the Milanos. I used to babysit for the Milanos, remember?"

I shook my head.

"Yes, you do, Mother! Mr. Milano was head of the chem lab in a cosmetic firm here in Clifton. He got razzed because his wife never wore make-up."

"Oh, that one. Little and dark-haired; pretty. I remember. She didn't need make-up."

"Right. Well, this woman"—Ellen tapped the enlargement with the back of her forefinger—"rented the house next door, furnished. Her husband was in the Army."

"Did you ever see him?"

"No. He was stationed in Germany. Then the marriage broke up."

"Did Mrs. Milano tell you that?"

"She must have. I heard it somewhere. Anyway, one day Mrs. Milano and the neighbors realized that nobody was living there anymore. The house was empty."

"Before or after the baby?"

"Before, I'm sure. I remember Mrs. Milano saying she hoped the poor girl had a mother to go home to. She wondered about her for a long time."

"I can imagine. Do you have any more?"

"Plenty, upstairs. All the old neighborhood. I was saving for my Leica that summer. I did a lot of babysitting."

"I mean of this particular neighbor."

"This is all I've found so far."

"May I have it?"

"Certainly. That's why I blew it up; made the prints."

Upstairs again, we spent the next hour at the dining table, going over those photographs Ellen had taken during her high school years. Some were neatly filed in albums; most were jumbled piles in shoe boxes or limp brown envelopes. Some of the faces I remembered; some had been completely forgotten. But not one other shot of the young woman I was convinced was the long-ago Julie.

"Ellen, you were always photographing the little Milano girl. You must have given some of the best shots to Mrs. Milano."

"The Milanos aren't here anymore. He was transferred to the west coast the week our twins were born."

"Don't you have their address?"

"Well, yes. That is, I *did* have their address."

"I see." Silence. "We could always find them, trace them through his company. Is anybody we used to know still living on the circle?"

"I don't know. I haven't been back there since Dad was transferred to Pennsylvania. We could drive over to Plains tomorrow if you want to."

That's what we did. After Ellen had prepared lunch, so the sitter wouldn't have to do it, we drove down Route 46 to 23; made the turn-off.

It was a long tree-shaded street, ending in the ample cul-de-sac where we used to live. The blue spruce I'd had planted in the front yard was tall now, handsome, reaching for the sky. The house itself was white, and the moss green shutters had been taken away. The house used to be a soft pale yellow.

Ellen drove slowly around the circle, watchful of kids approaching on their bikes. "Do you want to knock on doors?"

"It wouldn't accomplish anything." The whole area looked different. "Do you remember where the Milanos lived?"

"Back this way, seven or eight houses down. We just passed it. There's a screened-in side porch, and a red Japanese maple out front. I remember when Mrs. Milano had it put in. Ah—here." She stopped the car midway between what used to be the Milano house, and the house next door. "Trigger any memories?"

"Kind of. I used to see Julie wandering around out front here once in a while. Or sitting on the steps, buffing her nails. She wore gold-rimmed glasses."

"And her hair was very long and very blond." Ellen sighed, then chuckled at her sixteen-year-old self. "Except for her lumpy middle, I thought she was the most glamorous thing I'd ever seen."

"Those were the days," I murmured absently. Then: "I used to see a man around once in a while. Do you remember him?"

"Oh, sure. He was a relative, I think. Not too big; shiny black hair. He was always working around the yard."

"Did you ever talk to him?"

"Only once that I remember. I was taking some pictures of the Milano child and her puppy, and he came over and asked me not to point my camera into his yard."

"What did you do?"

"I said okay, and changed position, and shot from another angle."

"Was he unpleasant about it?"

"No, he was nice enough. He always said hi, and he helped me catch the puppy once. That day, I guess I just thought the neighbor woman didn't want to be photographed because she was pregnant."

"But in that photo she looked as if she were sleeping. She couldn't have objected."

Ellen lifted her shoulders. "Women feel that way, especially when they're close to term. Probably he knew it."

More than likely. I looked around at the houses I must

have passed hundreds of times in years gone by. Only eight years ago, and not one of them looked familiar. I said, "You must have babysat for more than one family on this street."

"I did, but the Milanos were my steadies. There was a family right along here, matter of fact, across the street." She shifted, and backed slowly. "That's the house, I remember the weather vane, but the people probably—" She was looking at the mailboxes on the left. "Yup. Tully. That's the name." She stopped the car; looked at me questioningly.

"I don't know," I said. A woman in faded shorts and halter was on her knees digging in a flower bed along the driveway. A girl with the long thin tanned legs of a ten- or eleven-year-old was walking away from her toward the open double door of the garage. I could see a red Toyota, a bike, a rack of tools. "What would we say?"

Not answering, Ellen shifted again and pulled the car to the left, stopping at the end of the driveway. She rolled down the window. "Hi. Mrs. Tully?"

"Yes?" The woman straightened, pushing back short-cropped brown hair with a gloved hand. She had a round pleasant face.

"I'm Ellen Pelham. I used to live down on the circle"— Ellen was getting out of the car, leaving the door open— "and I used to babysit for you and the Milanos."

"Well, Ellen, for heaven's sake!" She got to her feet, taking off her gloves as she came down the driveway. "I'd know you anywhere." They shook hands. "How nice to see you! Whatever brought you back to this neck of the woods?"

Ellen laughed. "I don't live that far away. Clifton. My mother's here on a visit, and we were driving around and saw you—"

"You remembered me after all this time! My goodness." Flushed with pleasure, she came down to the car, bent and thrust in a square tanned hand. "Mrs. Pelham, I've often told the story of our rummage sale fiasco."

"Oh, you have, have you?" I smiled. I didn't remember it.

"Will you ever forget how we scurried when the rains came? The weatherman had promised we'd be safe using the church yard for our overflow and then that sudden storm—"

Now I remembered. I laughed along with her.

"Can't you come in? It's so good to see you. I have some iced tea. Ellen, why don't you pull your car in the drive and we'll—"

It was almost noon now, and the heat was building. The living room was cool and dim. "I draw the draperies the minute I get up in the morning," Mrs. Tully explained, "and open them at night. How would you like some tuna salad? I made it early this morning so the seasonings should be through it by now."

"Oh," Ellen said, "we can't; we have children to get back to." Then, seeing Mrs. Tully's disappointment: "How about some of that iced tea?"

"Great. There's plenty. I like it, too."

Mrs. Tully turned toward the kitchen, faded blue shorts tight over firm, chunky thighs. Her square back and shoulders were tanned in varying degrees, souvenirs of the different gardening tops she wore.

"Do you still keep the potato chips in the big red canister?" Ellen asked, following.

"Yes, I still do." Mrs. Tully chuckled, pleased that Ellen remembered. "Red for danger. Calories."

I could hear them laughing, chattering, out there in the kitchen; the crunch of an ice-cube tray being emptied. Ellen was talking about her twins; Mrs. Tully about her own two, a boy and a girl. Not twins, thank God; six years apart.

I leaned back in the comfortable club chair and looked around. On top of the television console were framed photographs of the Tully children: light brown hair, blue eyes. I gazed appreciatively at a tilt-top desk, pine and curly maple, and at a high cherry wood china closet. The top shelf behind the curving glass was filled with sparkling cut glass; the second held a collection of pink lusterware and a few serving pieces of delicate-looking china. In one corner of that second shelf, on a teakwood stand, was a small dessert plate that looked familiar. I got up to look at it, and that was when Mrs. Tully returned, Ellen trailing.

"I was admiring your cut glass," I said. "My mother always said it would come into fashion again. My daughters have some of the pieces now."

"And love them." Ellen handed me a tinkling glass of tea. "What's more beautiful than a sparkling cut-glass bowl filled with cranberry sauce at holiday time?"

"My grandmother used to say the same thing." Mrs. Tully put a bowl of chips and a plate of macaroons down on the cocktail table. "This all was hers." She came over to stand beside me.

I pointed to the second shelf. "Beautiful, this pitcher. It's eighteenth century, isn't it?"

"Most people wouldn't have known." She smiled. "Are you a collector?"

"Not really. But it's lustered inside and out." I started to turn away. Then: "That plate. I think I've seen one like it before."

Mrs. Tully laughed depreciatingly. "I doubt it. It isn't anything. I keep it for sentimental reasons."

"Your mother painted it? Your grandmother?"

"Heavens, no. They hadn't an artistic bone in their bodies; neither do I. This plate was given to me by my music teacher in high school. Some of us wanted to get into the band, but we weren't good enough. Miss Carlyle promised if we'd practice faithfully and made it to the tryouts, she'd give us a reward. This was it."

Ellen laughed. "At that age, a hand-painted piece of china must have been some reward."

"Nobody was thrilled," Mrs. Tully admitted ruefully. She sat down next to Ellen on the sofa, pushing the potato chips Ellen's way. "The boys smashed their plates the minute they were out of sight of school. Most of the girls took theirs home." She sighed and smiled a little. "But Miss Carlyle was a good old soul."

"What school was that?" I asked.

"Bainbridge."

"We drove past our old house," Ellen said. "Are you the only family left in the neighborhood? Since we lived here?"

"Just about. You know of course the Milanos are in California."

"Yes. What about any of the other neighbors? Do you hear from any of them?"

"Not anymore. People write once or twice, if that, after they move away, and that's it. There have been so many."

"There was one—" Ellen leaned forward, reaching for a potato chip. "I used to see her a lot when I sat for the Milanos, and for you. I've often wondered about her."

"Who was that?"

"I forget her name. She was a blonde, quite young and very pregnant."

Mrs. Tully smiled. "That doesn't help much. Most of us went streaked-blond that year, and some of us were very pregnant."

"This neighbor wasn't streaked," Ellen said. "She was golden-blond. Her husband was stationed in Germany. Don't you remember her? She lived right across the street."

Silence. Mrs. Tully looked thoughtful. "Yes, I guess I do. Vaguely. I didn't know her though. I don't think we even spoke all the time she lived here."

She put her iced tea down on the table. The glass clicked.

Another short silence. I said, "Do the same people still own that house next to the Milanos?"

"No, the original owners rented it out for a few years while deciding where to retire. It's been sold twice since then. This neighborhood has been a gold mine for the real estate people. Where are you living now, Mrs. Pelham?"

"Pennsylvania."

"Oh, yes. Beautiful state." She didn't ask where in Pennsylvania.

Somehow the warmth had gone out of our reunion.

On the way home Ellen was quiet.

"What's the matter?"

She frowned. "I babysat with the neighbors' kids all through high school. That was four years of babysitting. Yet when I was inquiring about the blonde, she said 'that' year, as if she knew exactly the particular time I referred to."

"She said she was pregnant. We all remember the year we were pregnant, the maternity clothes we couldn't wait to put on and couldn't wait to get out of."

"Yes, but she said she didn't know that woman, that she never even spoke to her. I didn't ask her, remember; she volunteered that information."

"So she did."

"I used to sit out on the screened-in side porch after I put the little Milano girl to bed, in the dark mostly, listening to my records."

"Yes, I remember your toting your record-player everywhere."

"I saw Mrs. Tully go into that house next door more nights than I can tell you. Mrs. Tully didn't feel well, and spent most of her days in bed. But whenever her husband was away—and that was often—she always was over there."

Ellen slowed for a red light. She looked at me. "Mother, Mrs. Tully knew that neighbor, and she knew her well. She lied. Why?"

11

I took the seven o'clock plane back to Harrisburg, and when I pulled in our driveway it was dusk. There were no lights in the house which meant Walt had gone from the office directly to the club. He'd have dinner there, or I hoped so. A BLT would do me fine.

Leaving the car in the drive, I stepped out into the heat. How many days, weeks, of it had we had? I went around the garage and through the side gate to the garden. It was very quiet. It always was when our neighbors were away. Where were the crickets? Ah, there one was. Then another, and another.

Tomorrow morning, no matter what the temperature, I'd get out here and do something about this jungle. I tore a fat cucumber from the vine, and a clump of lettuce from the ground, and took them over to the back steps. Dusk was deepening. A small creature rustled somewhere. A rabbit probably. I hoped it was outside the stockade; not in.

For forty-five minutes, the entire flight, I'd held a good murder mystery in my hands, and I couldn't remember one page of what I'd read.

I went back to the tall lush plants along the fence, and chose two plump tomatoes. They fell into my hands, still warm from the fading day's sun. I started to straighten, slipping one into the left patch pocket of my overblouse, the other into the right. Did I need another? Walt often ate a plump, juicy one, chilled and halved and salted, with his breakfast.

Something touched my head. I started, brushed at my hair. Those rose bushes. Neglected, out of control now, they were climbing over to this side of the fence.

Yes, one more tomato.

I reached over and down, careful not to hit a stake, parting the fragrant vines with my hands. It was too dark now to see in there. The first one, more than ready, slipped away from my fingertips. I felt deeper into the plant for another. It fell plump and smooth and warm into my palm.

Again, as I straightened, something touched my head. Which of the wandering roses? I looked up.

The thing was white, only a few inches from my face. My heart jumped.

It was a hand. A hand white in the darkening, groping, groping.

"No—" I started to back away.

It kept reaching, a blind thing, silently groping for my head.

Another step back. I slipped, caught myself. Something squished slippery under my heel.

I stared at that suspended thing, that white, groping hand.

Then I whirled and ran.

12

"Where've you been?" Walt said.

"Out in the garden."

"You left the front door open."

"No, I didn't."

"Wide open. Have a good trip?" He kissed me. "Your teeth are chattering."

I handed him a tomato.

"You squeezed it," he said. "It's dripping."

I reached into my patch pockets, handed him the other two.

He took them. "Hey, you're trembling! What happened?"

I told him. Oh, how good to see his car in the drive behind mine! Oh, how wonderful to see the lights on in our house, to know he was there. I told him over and over about that white hand touching my head, reaching over the fence out of nowhere, groping, groping—

"Honey, calm down." He juggled the tomatoes, put an arm around me. "The hand would have seemed whiter in the dark. Could even have been a glove."

"I don't know. I don't think so. It was a hand, a silent, dead-white, awful hand."

"Okay, okay. Come on."

We put the tomatoes in the refrigerator. Walt turned on

the outside light and brought the lettuce and cucumber in from the back steps. We went out into the garden. I told him what I had done, showed him precisely where I had been standing.

Walt shook his head, his eyes going around the fence. He went over to close the gate. Suddenly he turned. "Maybe somebody's in trouble out there. Somebody cutting through—a heart attack, or a seizure of some kind."

He hurried up the back steps into the kitchen, grabbing the flashlight from the telephone table, then went down through the garage to the other side of the fence. I followed. He was flashing the light along the fence, then out over the grounds. He flashed it into the yard next door as he walked, and into the yard behind.

"I would have heard any call for help," I said as he came back toward me. "It was quiet."

"Sometimes they can't call out," he said.

"People who are choking can't," I said. "That's how you know they're choking, and not having a heart attack."

Moving slowly now, Walt flashed the light on the ground along the fence. "There was someone here all right. Look at that." The deep mulch had been trampled, each footprint obliterating the next. The climbing roses had rambled past their trellises, but none had wandered over the fence. "Whoever was here has a few scratches to show for it."

"Not if he was wearing enough clothes."

"Why do you say 'he'?" Walt asked quickly.

"This fence is five feet high. What woman we know could reach way over it?"

"Whoever it was didn't reach very far over, just enough

to touch your head. You're five-seven; more, in heels.
There must have been an arm attached to that hand."

"I don't remember an arm," I said.

I stopped at my car to pick up my handbag and the
brown envelope of photos Ellen had given me. Back in
the house I put the bacon on low. Walt had had dinner a
couple of hours ago, but for him a BLT was dessert.
While the lettuce was crisping in ice water, I showed him
the prints of the Milano neighbor I'd brought from Ellen's. They didn't mean anything to him. "I don't remember her," he said. "Doubt if I ever saw her."

I said, "You accused me of leaving the front door open.
I hadn't been in the house. I went directly from the car to
the garden. And the door wasn't open when I drove in. I
would have noticed."

He looked up. "Right." He nodded. "You, you would
have noticed."

I turned the bacon, and we went through the house.
There was nothing; everything was the same.

"Why would anyone come into our house, not take a
thing, leave by the front door, and come around to the
outside of the fence, and try to scare me to death?"

"Almost did. Also distracted you."

We looked at each other. "Two of them," I said.

"Could have been."

"They knew somehow that I was away, and that you
weren't here. One was watching, and when I drove in—"

"Could have been that way," Walt said.

We went down to the kitchen and had our bacon, lettuce and tomato sandwiches on whole-wheat toast, with
glasses of cold milk.

What was in our house that somebody had to have?

13

I don't know when Walt contacted him, but the next morning at ten Chief Henderson was over to admire my roses. I went out with him, carrying pruning shears. "No heel marks," he pointed out when I showed him the spot. "Must have been wearing flat-soled sandals, or well-worn sneakers. Any other places around the fence?"

"No, only here between these two bushes. It's all heavily mulched. I've found it pays."

"So my wife says. She's big on glads."

We walked around the fence anyway. The Chief agreed: the rest of the mulch had not been disturbed.

"Did this hand you saw have a ring attached to it, or a watch, or a bracelet?"

"No. Wouldn't I remember?"

"Hard to say. It was dark. You were startled, frightened."

"My unconscious would have remembered," I said. "There was only a white hand."

"Somebody was wearing black then, long-sleeved. A lookout would wear black."

I cut a bouquet of scarlet roses for Chief Henderson's wife, and took him into the kitchen while I wrapped the stems in dampened peat moss and wax paper. He asked about the photos I'd brought back from Ellen's. "Taken about eight years ago?"

"No, nearer ten. We moved down here when Ellen was in her first year of college. These were taken the summer between her sophomore and junior years at high school."

He looked at the prints, and went back to the one Ellen had thought the clearest, most telling. Julie, a younger Julie, lying on a chaise longue, face to the sun. "Same one, I'd say. I saw her in profile too. The same; but different."

He meant not that young anymore, soaking up the sun; but lying the same way, on her back, face turned to merciless lights, on that table in the hospital morgue. "Did anybody know you'd be away the last two days?"

"Penny Wilde; Eleanor Brock. I often go to New Jersey."

"Anybody know when you were expected back?"

"Walt knew I'd be in sometime last night, but he didn't know when. I wasn't sure which flight I'd be taking when I called him at the office. He didn't have to meet me, I had my car, so he said he'd play his eighteen holes as usual."

"And he did." A statement.

I nodded. "And he did. Everybody knows Walt's golf schedule." Then: "There weren't any trash cans in Julie Gordon's house."

"No, there weren't, except for that empty wastebasket upstairs. What brought that up?"

"Most people, if there's no disposal in the kitchen, keep some kind of container in the cupboard under or near the sink. If there's no compactor somewhere—in the basement, or garage—there's usually a garbage can outside. I didn't think of it until later. I almost called you back about it the other day, and about something else."

"Why didn't you?"

"I figured if any mail was delivered to Julie Gordon's house, you'd know about it." No response. I handed him the roses. "If you put them on the floor of your car, they'll keep fresh until you get home. Don't forget them."

"I won't."

"Who would steal a garbage can?"

"It's possible it wasn't stolen."

I remembered Naomi May's account of that early morning departure: *They had a lot of junk in the back seat.* Probably she'd told Chief Henderson the same thing. I said, "You think Julie and that man took a trash can away with them when they left?"

"Highly possible."

"With a newborn baby in it? Dead?"

"That's occurred to us, but in all probability Julie was still carrying the baby herself. The container, or containers, were filled with household and personal belongings. Remember, that house was pretty empty when you consider two people had been living there for six months."

"That would explain that, wouldn't it?" I supposed the Chief was hoping I wouldn't start that *what-happened-to-the-baby? why-hasn't-it-been-found?* routine. He was getting enough of that in the newspapers. I said, "Even the *TV Guide*s hadn't come by mail, I noticed; they must have been picked up at market or a magazine stand."

"At market," Chief Henderson said, "every week."

"Not a personal thing in that house except for the plate."

"What plate?"

"It was on the first shelf of the kitchen cupboard. I remember it because it was hand-painted, and all the other things were plastic. I think I saw a similar one yesterday."

"You think?"

"It looked like it. If I could see the one at Julie's house again . . ."

So we went out to the car, tenderly stowed Mrs. Henderson's roses under the front seat and, on our way to Julie Gordon's house, I told him about Ellen's and my visit to the old neighborhood in Plains. "Mrs. Tully just laughed about the plate when I remarked on it," I said. "My daughter Ellen is sure Mrs. Tully and that young woman in the photos knew each other."

Julie Gordon's house was the same. Quiet, waiting; nothing changed. In the kitchen, the pad was still in place next to the telephone. I reached into the cupboard for the hand-painted dessert plate. Pine tree; pine cones. A blue sky. "Very much like the one I saw at Mrs. Tully's."

"Signed?"

"With flourishes, see?" I held up the plate. "It's MLC, or possibly WLQ. What do you think?"

"Don't ask me. Was this Mrs. Tully's plate signed?"

"I couldn't see. It was in a china closet."

"Where was her high school?"

"Bainbridge, she said. New Jersey. I never heard of it. Can we go upstairs while we're here?"

He nodded. I put the plate back on the shelf. On the

stairs, I said, "The plates may not mean a thing. There was a period years ago when little old ladies took painting lessons every Tuesday and Thursday afternoon at the Y.W.C.A. They all ended up painting the same things over and over, stiff-looking, and all alike. Except for the signatures you couldn't tell one would-be artist's work from another's."

Chief Henderson chuckled. "My Aunt Anna's house is full of stuff like that."

In Julie's bedroom, I turned back the candlestick spread, and the sheets that never had been used. "The mattress is spotless."

"She bought it only six months ago," the Chief said. "What did you expect?"

"A mattress pad. A new mattress, ergo a new mattress pad. Any woman can tell you."

"She didn't take that kind of interest."

"Something like this, I think she did. I bet there was a mattress pad on this bed, and I'd say a heavy-duty rubber sheet too. That could have been part of the trash-container cargo they took away with them, including a pillow and linens from the other room and bath. Or, no, not the pillow. Julie was using that on the front seat. Naomi May said she was leaning against one." I looked at him. "I have a feeling the baby was born right here."

He wasn't surprised. "It could have been."

I turned back to smooth the bed. He and his people had been over this room thoroughly, again and again. Which was why I was being given free rein. *Any possible source is not overlooked.* Another thing he'd said at the Soroptimist Club meeting.

"Anything else?" he asked.

I shook my head. On our way out I paused and slid the mirrored closet door open. There on the floor was the blue weekend bag, and the smaller case. "What was in them?"

"Couple of tags. Just as they came from the store."

I looked up at the shelf. "What happened to the wig stands?"

"The lab guys have them."

I waited. Nothing. Darn him! *I tell you everything I know, everything I can think of, and you—*

"It was a man's wig, Ida; the gray one that was here."

A man with shaggy gray hair. "When I saw that closet in there"—I nodded toward the next room—"it was the way it had been left, wasn't it? No white jacket, no—"

"That was the way we found it. Not even an empty suitcase."

"Naomi May—she's the one who lives next door—"

"I know Naomi May."

"She said that man who stayed with Julie used to be away until very late at night sometimes. Could he have been part of a catering service?"

"Doubtful, but we're still checking. You're thinking of the man you saw cleaning up after the Brocks' party."

"Yes. Remember I told you about a conversation I listened in on? I told you I thought the voices came from the solarium?"

"You said there was only a gray-haired man there when you went in."

"I know it, but I've been thinking. There are three glass doors out of that solarium. Just because that man said he'd been alone those last fifteen minutes doesn't mean he was. He could have been one of the two I heard talking."

"Could have been, but what did you hear? A squabble between two people checking up on each other."

"No, more than that! Remember I said the woman suddenly stopped talking? Then she said, 'You better get home.' Remember I said I thought I heard a gasp?"

He nodded. "I remember."

"Could she have stopped talking because all of a sudden she knew she was going into labor? 'You better get home', she said. I couldn't swear on a Bible that Julie was the one I saw in the driveway when we arrived at the Brock party, but whoever it was surely looked like her from the back."

"You didn't recognize the voices." A statement.

"No. They were low, angry, fierce; that's all."

"The woman you saw in the driveway was wearing a white dress; she was tall and dark-haired, and you'd been thinking of Julie Gordon."

"Well, yes." I looked away. That was true.

"Did you see anyone at the Brock party that tall, with long black hair, wearing a white dress?"

"No. No, I didn't."

"We haven't found anyone who did."

"Oh?" I lifted my head. "Did you check with Eleanor Brock?"

"Especially with Eleanor Brock. We went all the way down the guest list."

"Then it must have been Julie I saw." I slid the closet door closed. "And the timing would fit, wouldn't it? The baby was born Saturday night. It must have been born here because why is all the linen gone? And early Sunday morning they took the baby somewhere. Naomi May saw them drive out."

"So she said. They couldn't have gone far."

"No, because they were back here Sunday." And dead Sunday night, I thought.

He was thinking the same thing. "Come on," he said, "let's go."

On the way downstairs, I said, "It's been driving me nuts, wondering why my address was on Julie's telephone pad, why she drove past my house; why she turned up at Penny Wilde's get-together that Saturday. Maybe I have an idea."

"What's that?"

"What if, after Julie and that man moved here, she heard my name or Walt's? What if, for some reason, she didn't want to be recognized, but thought she might be? What if, after finding where we lived, she kept driving down our street hoping to get a glimpse of us, to see if we were the same Pelhams who had lived in Plains? What if, when we met at market, she couldn't be sure?" I paused at the bottom of the stairs. "Know why she couldn't be sure?"

"Why?"

"Because in Plains, I was heavier, my hair was dark and sculptured-cut—"

"Whatever that means."

"—but now, I'm ten pounds lighter, my hair is silvery-gray, and it's swept back and up, making me taller."

"Okay, so you're thinner and taller than she remembered, different coloring, and that's why she came to the

Wildes'. She had to talk to you. Sounds plausible, except she must have already known you'd moved here from Plains. There was Mrs. Smith along with all the other neighbors who meet and talk at the shopping plaza every day."

"Yes, but what she wanted to know was did *I* remember her."

His hand on my elbow, the Chief urged me out.

"Why me?" I asked. "Instead of the Brocks, or the Wildes? They lived in Plains at the same time too."

"You said they claim they never knew her."

"Neither did I."

Chief Henderson locked the front door with the labeled key. He looked at me. "Bainbridge, huh?"

I nodded. "That's what Mrs. Tully said."

One minute after Chief Henderson dropped me off, I was dialing Ellen's number.

14

Penny Wilde came wheeling up the driveway next morning as I was rounding the outside fence. She was pink and peeling, and wearing bright red shorts. "Have a nice visit with your daughter?"

"Dandy."

"You weren't gone long." She parked her bike, kicked the stand. "What are you doing?"

"Cutting back my roses to toddlers' size."

"How come? You never do it until fall." She followed me, picking up the clippings with careful fingers, putting them gingerly into the oval wicker basket on the ground. "How long is this going to take?"

"I intend to tackle the whole shebang. Why?"

"I thought maybe you'd go with me to see the new baby down the block. She's the one you just went in on with us for a present. Beautiful, I hear."

"I can't today, Penny."

"We'd stay just a few minutes. The new father left for Harrisburg this morning. He'll be away two days. The new mother is panicking already, and he hasn't been gone three hours."

"There are friends, neighbors. She'll be all right."

"So you're all tied up for the day, huh?"

"I think I'm going to be."

"Did you hear the police have a line on Harlon Pierce?"

"No." I didn't look up. Chief Henderson had not mentioned that to me yesterday, nor to Walt either so far as I knew. "It's not his real name," I said.

"No, and I said it wasn't, remember?"

"I remember."

"There was nothing in the papers last night; I heard it this morning. He worked in a nursing home years ago. His last name was Quick. They traced the fingerprints. A fingerprint, Mrs. Smith said."

"Mrs. Smith told you?"

"At market. She and Margaret."

"Where'd they hear it?"

"Margaret knows somebody down at the hospital. She was a nurse before she retired."

"Around here?"

"New York State, I think. Maybe New York City. She's Mrs. Smith's niece."

"Have you known her long?"

"Since I was little. She used to visit. Then when Mrs. Smith broke her hip, Margaret came back to stay."

"Mrs. Smith doesn't have any children of her own?"

"Only one son who was killed in the war. She was widowed young. She needs Margaret now. It's worked out fine for both."

Penny didn't stay long. When we turned the back corner of the fence, she'd had it. "I'm just not the outdoor type," she said apologetically as she reached for her peeling shoulders. She had scratches all over her arms.

Walt didn't come home for lunch. Around one, Eleanor

Brock called. Would I like to drive to the Poconos with her this afternoon to see the new baby?

"Thanks, but I can't today."

"A true Brock," Eleanor said. "Blond, blue-eyed." She hoped, she added darkly, the daughter-in-law's mother didn't think she was keeping that baby up *there*.

I suspected Eleanor was looking for moral support while invading enemy territory, but I'd seen the two ladies in action before. Mother of the bride; mother of the groom. I wanted no part of it.

I finished my lunch and went out to lug the rest of the rose bush clippings to the compost pile behind the tool house. The mail had come. There was the Philadelphia paper, two catalogs, identical, from the same mail order house, the telephone bill, and a legal-sized envelope, the address childishly hand-printed in pencil.

I cut it open with a kitchen knife. Inside there was a single sheet of lined paper, folded once, lengthwise. The same childish-looking, penciled printing:

FORGET JULIE GORDON. LET HER REST IN PEACE. OR YOU TOO SHALL DIE. THIS IS A WARNING!

This is a warning.

I read it again, then turned the lined sheet of paper over. Nothing on the back.

I looked at the envelope. Postmarked New York, N.Y. But the bottom of the circle faded out. Part of July I could see, but not the date.

What difference did it make? Everybody we knew went to New York now and then, or Philadelphia, or Boston, or—

The date makes a lot of difference! New York mail takes only a day!

I tilted the envelope against the light. I couldn't read that circle. There was nothing there to read. I looked at the lined sheet of paper again, then folded it and slipped it into the slitted envelope.

Chief Henderson would be interested in this, and I would see that he got it.

I was sitting at the kitchen table with a road atlas trying to find Bainbridge, New Jersey, when Ellen telephoned. "I went yesterday afternoon."

"How'd it go?"

"She'd just come in from somewhere. She was dressed for town. But, Mother, if she'd seen me coming she wouldn't have opened the front door. She's afraid of me."

"Of you? My dear."

"Well, she's afraid of something. How different from last time! If I hadn't lied, she wouldn't have let me in."

"What did you lie about, Ellen?"

"Not actually a lie. You've been saying for years you wanted to open an antique shop, fine old china and glass."

"And I've thought for years nobody was listening."

"So I told Mrs. Tully you were impressed with her collection of cut glass. I said you wondered if any of it was marked. She said cut glass wasn't marked, and I said *au contraire*, that you said some fine old pieces were marked dimly—pieces from the late eighteen hundreds. She was suspicious at first, then she got interested. She took the key off the top of the china cabinet and opened the glass door. And you know what?"

"What?"

"I think that compote has a mark at the bottom of the bowl part. I held it up to the light. Hardly distinguishable, but—"

"Sweetheart, that isn't why I asked you to go over there. Did you see the plate?"

"Yes. It's signed all right. The first of three initials looked like an M or a W. All curlicues. Two other interesting things."

"China?"

"No, listen. First, there'd been nothing about two small-town Pennsylvania murders in our local paper until two nights ago. It was toward the back of the last section. Just a small paragraph. The paper was on Mrs. Tully's sofa, opened to that page. You saw how neat she is."

"I noticed. So an old newspaper hadn't been chucked into the trash basket along with junk mail."

"I'd say, remembering, that's her habit. She never kept magazines either, for more than a day or two. There never was anything current to read around there. Second, and this is troubling, her daughter came in with a friend, asking if there was any ice cream in the freezer downstairs. Mrs. Tully blew her stack, ordering the kids out of the house. That couldn't have been a usual happening because first the little girl looked unbelieving, then as if she wanted to cry."

"Was this before or after you looked at the cut glass?"

"Before. I hadn't been there long. Incidentally, I'm sure she didn't see my eyes straying to either the newspaper on the sofa, or the dessert plate."

"Good. She must have wanted her daughter away from

you for some reason. How did Mrs. Tully seem when you left?"

"I think I left her suspecting I might be trying to pull a fastie on her cut glass. You know what they say about some antique dealers. Could be she's running all over town right now, trying to find out if she has some treasure she didn't know she owned."

I hoped that was all Mrs. Tully was worrying about.

"Ellen, I hesitate to tell you this—"

"You don't have to. Just let me know which flight."

"I'm doing it differently this time. But I'll be seeing you sometime tomorrow."

15

School was out of course, but I was hoping that part of the high school building would be open for summer make-up classes, or lessons in tennis or swimming. Surely there would be someone around in that little out-of-the-way village of Bainbridge.

The side roads, after leaving Route 80, had just as many pot holes as the side roads in Pennsylvania.

After asking directions of an elderly man walking a raccoon on a leash, I pulled up in front of a sprawling red-brick building. It was set back from the avenue, surrounded by a vast tree-shaded lawn. The sprinklers had been turned off, but the grass was still wet.

Starting up the wide middle walk, I noticed there were no cars. The heavy entrance doors had that closed-for-the-season look. I pushed against them, then pulled. They were unlocked.

I stepped into the dim coolness and stopped, smelling that school-building smell, waiting for my eyes to adjust. The sound of canned laughter came from somewhere.

Now I could see the high gray walls lined with gray lockers, and the black and white squares of the gleaming vinyled floor. Parked in the middle of the hall three doors down was a cleaning cart bristling with brooms and mops and brushes, and trailing polishing cloths. I started toward the open door. The custodian was eating lunch out of a small styrofoam container on the floor beside him, his feet up on the back of the seat ahead, eyes glued to a TV game show. Chuckling along with the audience, he didn't stir as I came in. "That you, Em?"

"No." He didn't hear me. "No," I said again loudly.

He turned, stretching his neck to look back at me. He swung his feet to the floor. "Who are you?"

"Ida Pelham. I'm a member of the National Historical Society; associate member of the Smithsonian." I slid the cards from the back of my wallet. "I'm interested in local history—"

"Oh, yeah?" Brightening, he wriggled his wizened frame out of the desk chair and, half a sandwich in hand, came up the aisle toward me. He glanced at the cards I held out, but didn't take them. "I'm a local history buff myself. Lived here all my life; know everything about everybody, the quick and the departed."

His roly-poly Em waddled in with a white insulated bag from Henri's Ice Cream Parlor. "Butterscotch chip today," she announced cheerily, eyes darting toward the TV screen. Then the small eyes swiveled back to me. "We know you from somewhere, don't we?"

"I don't think so." Introductions, explanations; pleasantries exchanged.

While watching the *Young and the Restless,* we shared the butterscotch chip out of paper cups. During the commercials, I learned that custodian Jenkins and his Em lived a block down from school, that they had no car and no children and didn't regret it the way things were today, and that they had visited the Smithsonian the summer of

'71. How ol' Lindy ever got over the ocean in that crate—

I kept reminding myself of Chief Henderson's key word at the Soroptimist dinner meeting: Patience.

While waiting for *Search for Tomorrow*, we talked about teachers. Of the two who painted china, ten or fifteen years ago—elderly, you know, not up with the times, but they had tenure—one had died in the summer of '74, just keeled over during the Fourth of July parade. The other, Miss Carlyle, still lived with her mother, who turned eighty-six this past April.

"Here in the village?"

"Just a few blocks down. The old homestead on Pershing."

The old homestead wasn't hard to find. It was square, white-painted, set a little farther back from the street than the other houses; more yard on either side. The front door opened as I started up the four wooden steps. "Ah, Mrs. Pelham. Mr. Jenkins telephoned, advising us to expect you."

Miss Carlyle was a gray-haired woman in her mid-sixties, tall and slender. She wore rimless glasses, and reminded me a little of pictures I'd seen of President Woodrow Wilson. "Mother will join us. We too are fascinated by the past. Anything we can do to help—"

She led me through the living room, through the oaken archway into a parlor made small by thin oriental rugs, an upright piano, curio cabinets, and a clutter of antique furniture. Shelves on two walls held books and hand-painted china on ebony stands, most signed with a familiar flourish.

I admired the hand-painted plates; the chocolate set. "I

think I used to know two of your former students. They spoke so fondly of you."

"Indeed? Who?"

"I never knew their maiden names. They each have a dessert plate you'd painted and signed for them. An award of some kind, I think."

"Yes, yes; I used to do that." Miss Carlyle nodded, thin cheeks pink with pleasure. "Incentive, you know. And they've kept their plates all these years? I'm so glad. What are their married names? Perhaps—"

"One is Tully. Mildred, as I remember. She was a neighbor of ours in Plains. She still lives there."

"Milly Sparks Tully!" I turned toward the voice trumpeting over my shoulder. The old lady was coming toward the archway on her hickory cane. Another, older, plumper Woodrow Wilson. "She married Agnes Tully's oldest boy after his first wife died. She'd been crazy about him since she was in third grade and he was a high school football hero. But she took right over with the baby, Agnes said; settled right down. It wasn't easy for such a young girl, especially with him away on the road so much."

"Come sit down, Mother," Miss Carlyle said. She turned back to me. "What about the other former student of mine?"

"Her first name was Julie, but—" I shook my head regretfully. "Can't recall the last name. She lived in Plains too for a while."

"Julie," Miss Carlyle said. "Julie." She looked at her mother. "I don't think I ever had a Julie, did I? I had a Jules, and a—"

"The two lived across the street from each other," I said. Then, a stab in the dark: "Evidently they'd been close friends for years, long before Plains. Julie was tall and blond, wore glasses."

"Tall and blond!" The two women said it almost in unison. "Much taller than Mildred Tully?" the younger one asked.

"Yes." I calculated, took a guess. "Almost a head taller."

"Jane Cowell!" Mrs. Carlyle plumped down, ruffling the rug with her cane as she settled back on the empire sofa. "See, Winifred, what did I tell you? All these years you've worried about her for nothing. I told you that girl neither needed nor deserved anybody's concern."

Miss Carlyle ignored her mother. "Is she happily married?"

"She seemed content the last time I saw her," I said cautiously.

"How many children does she have?"

I didn't like this. Obviously Miss Carlyle cared. "She was expecting a baby the last time I talked with her."

Miss Carlyle frowned. "Doesn't she have a child about —oh, fourteen or so?"

"Might be. I don't remember seeing one around her house, but I didn't know her very—"

"I told you!" Mrs. Carlyle looked at her daughter triumphantly. "Like a cat, that kind always lands on her feet."

"Who really knows?" Miss Carlyle went over to the tall windows, parting the glass curtains to look out. "Mildred and Jane were inseparable all through grade school. In high school they went out for band; so they could go to the away football games, I expect. I didn't care for what reason. Some of my students have become music lovers in spite of themselves. But when Jane Cowell was in her junior year she dropped out of band and a few weeks later so did Mildred."

"Jane dropped band because she had to leave school," Mrs. Carlyle said. "She was pregnant, and not even sixteen. There's one in every class, isn't there, Winifred?"

Winifred Carlyle didn't seem to hear. She turned, looking at me. "The sad part is that if it had happened today—just a few short years later, mind you—Jane wouldn't have had to give up her education, wouldn't have had to face—"

"Nonsense," the old lady said.

"Was she a good student?" I asked.

"No, but she could have been if she'd applied herself. She joined the drama club because Mildred did—Mildred was a born actress, I thought—but that didn't last long. Then she tried the swim club; she did better there. But I didn't give up on her, and I was just beginning to get through to her, or I thought I was, when—"

"Nonsense," the old lady said again. She straightened abruptly, turning, lifting her white head. "Would you like some punch, Mrs. Pelham?"

"Oh, no, thank you." I looked at my watch.

"I insist," Mrs. Carlyle said firmly. "All fresh fruits—oranges, bananas, peaches—with honey and strawberry yogurt. A meal in itself. We have a new blender."

"Yes, we do insist." Winifred Carlyle was suddenly cheerful. She looked five years younger. "It won't take me but a minute. All mixed. It's chilling in the refrigerator."

Mrs. Carlyle looked fondly after her daughter. Then she turned confidingly. "I wouldn't say this in her presence for the world, but I must warn you not to take anything she says too seriously. Winifred thinks she has a way with young people, that she's a born teacher." Mrs. Carlyle shook her head. "She isn't. She should have stuck to her art work. She'd be a somebody today, if she had listened to me."

I looked around the room at the shelves of handpainted china. Maybe Winifred Carlyle wasn't an artist; maybe she wasn't a teacher. But two of her students had cared enough to keep, to treasure for years, a memento of hers. A memento of her.

I wondered whose idea it had been, those flourishing signatures.

Winifred Carlyle came back with three tall shortstemmed glasses on a hand-painted wooden tray. A pine tree atop a hill, cones on the ground; blue sky.

"These are for sipping," she said after she'd served her mother. "We've been having one every day lately before lunch. Relaxing and healthful. Take a small taste." She watched me, eyes mischievous behind her rimless glasses. She looked *ten* years younger! "Delicious?"

Delicious it was. Rich and creamy and smooth. And spiked to the whiskers with rum.

"I'd like the recipe," I said.

"I can give you a basic, then take it from there. Improvise."

"I gather that's what you do."

She lifted her shoulders. "It helps. Has Mildred licked her weight problem?"

"She's a little chunky. Looked fine to me though. Nice tan."

"But not fat. That's good." Miss Carlyle nodded, satisfied. "She'd get terribly overweight, then starve herself. Once, and it was very hot that June, and she was very fat, I came upon her in the girls' room. She was holding up her skirt and fanning herself with the school paper. She was embarrassed and so was I. Her inner thighs got chafed, you see. She explained that."

"It never occurred to me, but of course that would be a problem."

"Yes. Well, I'm glad she's staying thinner now. I'm happy she kept my plate. And Jane Cowell? She's still tall and blond and slender?"

I sipped my punch. "When I saw her last, she had changed the color of her hair."

"Mine is mostly cracked ice," Mrs. Carlyle called out querulously.

"Sorry, Mother. There's more out there when you want it."

"I want it now. And no more ice, please."

Miss Carlyle put down her drink, barely touched, and went over to her mother. She disappeared with her mother's glass through the dining room archway.

"Winifred doesn't know I know it," her mother said in a loud whisper, mouthing her words behind her hand, "but I'm sure she puts a stick in it. That's why she gives me mostly ice."

"It's very good," I said. "The chipped ice is the final touch."

"Not if it's mostly chipped ice. I'm not that old."

Miss Carlyle came back with her mother's refilled glass. "Sip, Mother; don't gulp." We moved back toward the windows. "I'll give her lunch after this, and then she'll stretch out on the sofa and snooze."

"It's too hot for her outdoors anyway," I said. "You asked about Julie—Jane Cowell. You have no idea what she did after she left high school?"

"No. She stayed with her parents for a while. Then she went away."

"Before her baby was born, or after?"

"Before. About two months before. She never came back."

"Nobody knows where she is?"

"Well, I didn't until you told me. Her parents hear from her occasionally, I'm told. I can understand why she stays away. There were many children; the father out of a job a good part of the time. The mother worked as a cleaning woman when she wasn't on the verge of delivering again. Jane used to go with her to the big houses. I always thought that explained a good part of it."

"The father of the baby was from one of those big houses?"

"No." She shook her head. "I meant that's when she learned that all families didn't live the way hers did. But you're right; it could have been that way. Heaven knows those young men were after her, home from college or prep school, any time their parents weren't looking." She sighed. "No, it was a quiet secretive senior who constantly cut classes because of his toothaches. Dark-haired, always smelling of cigarettes when I met him in the halls. I don't know what the attraction was. How I hated it when I saw her with him."

"Maybe he wasn't really the father."

"Everyone said he was. The school nurse said he admitted it."

"What happened to him?"

"He worked in a gas station for a while, then a nursing home."

"Where is he now?"

"Nobody knows. He left the nursing home for a better job at another one somewhere."

Old Mrs. Carlyle had put down her glass. She was nodding sleepily on the sofa. "Winifred? Lunch time, Winifred—"

"Do you remember his name?" I asked.

"Quick," Winifred Carlyle said. "Benjamin Quick."

16

"How'd you make out?" Ellen came over to the driveway as I pulled in. She'd been weeding.

"Fine. I found Miss Carlyle."

"Good for you. I was afraid she had moved away or died. Was she any help?"

"Much. Julie and Mrs. Tully didn't become new friends in Plains. They'd known each other from way back, all through school."

"Well, sure. Friends from before anyway." Ellen opened the door and slid my overnight bag from the back seat. "They never were seen together in public, yet they were close enough to share evening after late evening. They had to know each other from somewhere else. Dad wants you to call him."

"I said I would when I got here." I opened the car windows against the heat, and we started across the lawn toward the house. "Do you remember when Mrs. Tully was pregnant with her daughter?"

"Vaguely. I remember Mrs. Milano remarking it was dangerous for any woman to get that much overweight during pregnancy, so much so that she had to take to a bed of her own."

"Was Mrs. Tully terribly overweight?"

"Every pregnant woman looked terribly overweight to

me in those days." Ellen opened the door and we went into the air-cooled house. "Mrs. Milano said she looked like a waddling tent."

Upstairs the twins were waking from their naps. We could hear crib sides rattling, then a plop, another plop.

"They've discovered they can climb out," Ellen said. "I'll take your bag up."

A waddling tent, Mrs. Milano had said. I thought of the red tin of potato chips in the Tully kitchen. How easy for a very fat woman to feign pregnancy, to move temporarily from the bed of her solicitous husband. No lying side by side in those later months, the mother and the father, hands touching as they felt together the movements of their unborn child.

Mildred Sparks Tully would have had no difficulty turning into a very fat woman. And didn't the sight of maternity clothes always play tricks on the eyes and mind of the beholder?

The children, still flushed from sleep, blue eyes bright, were wearing red scraps of swimming trunks. "I'll turn on the sprinklers," Ellen said after the twins and I exchanged greetings. "That'll keep them busy for a while."

We sat in the breakfast room, drinking iced coffee, watching the twins in the fenced-in section of the yard. They ran back and forth, laughing and shouting, from one whirling sprinkler to the other. Their sturdy butterscotch-tanned legs were a study in inexhaustible energy.

I said, "I suppose you don't know if Mrs. Tully had a local obstetrician."

Ellen shook her head. "Her baby was premature, that's all I remember."

"Sure?"

"Pretty sure. She hadn't been married too long, and her husband—he's in sales, I think—was away on business. The son, his, by a first marriage, was at camp. She had some relatives in Vermont."

"And the baby was born there."

"That's how I remember it."

I thought a minute, then pushed back my chair. "I'd better call your father."

Walt wasn't at the office, and, no, not out in the plant either, his secretary said.

"When he comes in then, Pat, will you give him a message, please? Tell him I'm here at Ellen's, and that I'll be home tomorrow afternoon."

"He's at the house now, Mrs. Pelham."

"Now?" I glanced up at Ellen's cuckoo clock. "Why? Isn't he feeling well?"

"Oh, he's fine. Something went wrong with the wiring in your house, or— I don't really know. He just took off."

I pressed the cradle button, holding it down a few seconds, then dialed home. Walt answered on the fifth ring.

"Walt, why are you there? What's the matter?"

"It's all right. Everything's under control. The fire's out."

"Fire! What fire? Our house?"

"No, no. Only the garage; minimal damage. One of Henderson's men was driving by and saw the smoke."

"What happened?"

"We don't know yet."

"Pat said something about wiring."

"That's what they're looking into now."

"I'll come home."

"Not tonight; not in late afternoon traffic."

"Early tomorrow then," I said.

"That's better. Nothing to worry about. Nobody was hurt."

"Yes, well, that's the important thing."

But I was restless after I hung up; uneasy. I didn't know what to do with myself. We had an early dinner, Ellen's husband telephoned from Detroit, I read the twins *Honey Bear* and *Corky*, and at six-thirty I said, "I'd like to see Mrs. Tully again."

Ellen didn't want me to go. "Dad doesn't like you driving through the heavy traffic around here at night."

"I'll be back before then."

There were two cars in the Tully garage, a gray one next to the red Toyota. A rider-mower crisscrossed the driveway.

Mr. Tully, in his late forties, gray-haired, answered the door. He was a stocky man, fleshed out in front, barefooted, and wearing green plaid shorts and a faded shirt. "She's in the back yard, working in her garden."

"Oh, good. One of the neighbors thought she might be in the city."

"That was a couple of days ago. She didn't stay long. It's hotter'n hell down there." Newspaper in one hand, he leaned forward to open the screen door with the other. "Here. Come on through the house."

I could hear the muted roar of the dishwasher in the kitchen. "No, that's all right, thanks. I'll walk around."

"Whatever you say. Notice that side yard out there," he said. "All Mildred's doing."

He watched me off the stone steps. As I rounded the side and went past the opened windows, I heard the rapid clicks of a dial, then the instant sound of television.

Between the edge of the cobblestone walk and the house foundation, there was a low length of glinting white rock garden, bejewelled with delicate ferns and exquisite miniature roses. All his wife's doing, Mr. Tully had said.

She was on her knees, blue shorts and tank top blending with the bed of pink to purple pansies.

"Evening, Mrs. Tully," I called out. "Beautiful rock garden I just passed."

She looked up over her shoulder, then twisted, sitting back on her heels, the claw cultivator in her hand. "Why are you here?"

"Just stopped by."

"No." She shook her head. "You didn't just stop by. What do you want?"

"To talk."

"About what?"

"Well, you—I—" I was disconcerted. I hadn't expected this.

She stayed where she was, looking up at me, waiting.

"Mrs. Tully, we've got to talk about it."

"You and your daughter are going to ruin my life, do you know that?"

"No," I said. "Never."

"Yes. You are going to take away from me everything I ever loved." Her left hand was a fist on her knee, her right tight around the cultivator. "Will that make you happy?"

"It would break my heart." I meant it. "Please. If we—"

"The police were here today," she said harshly. "What made them come here?"

"Did you think they wouldn't come?" I tried to speak quietly, gently. "Sooner or later? They check, they trace—"

"Who started them? Who made sure they'd end up here?" Tea-brown eyes were hard, shiny. "I suppose you've already talked to my husband."

"Just to ask if you were home. He said you were out here."

"Did you tell him who you are?"

"Yes, and he pretended he remembered when I used to live here in Plains. He didn't, of course. He was dying to turn on the pre-game show. The Phillies are playing Cincinnati tonight."

"That's all?"

"That's all."

She didn't believe me. She said evenly, too evenly, "I want you to go away and never come back to this house again."

"I can't. Not quite yet. Mrs. Tully, Mildred, I have to talk with you."

"Well, I don't have to talk to you!"

"I think you do." Not liking it much, I reached into my handbag for the legal-sized envelope with its childish printing. I held it between thumb and forefinger, moving it slowly up and down, up and down. "A death threat by way of the U.S. mail is a federal offense."

A small strangled sound in her throat.

It came swiftly, that clawed thing. I pulled my foot. Not quite in time.

My handbag plopped to the grass.

Mildred Tully stared at the cultivator pinning down the tip of my sandal.

Then she began to cry.

17

"Mom? Are the strawberry popsicles done yet?"

"In the freezer."

Three little girls in bikinis, perspiring, had come biking up the side yard.

"Laurie wants pineapple."

"There's a pineapple left from yesterday."

Mildred Tully hadn't turned her head. She'd sounded almost cheerful. Her face was wet with tears.

I waited until the children had gone in the back way before I bent to pull two prongs of the cultivator from the tip of my sandal.

"I don't know what's the matter with me." Mrs. Tully wiped at her cheeks with the backs of her hands. "What if I had hit one of your veins, or an artery?"

"Well, you didn't." There was no pain, but I looked down at my foot anyway. No blood. "So that part's over." I picked up my handbag, and the white envelope that had slithered away.

Mrs. Tully didn't move, didn't say anything. I didn't put the white envelope away. I stood there, holding it. Finally I said, "Somebody killed Julie."

"Jane, her name was."

"Yes. Jane Cowell."

"She didn't like it. Plain Jane, she said. She always wanted to be a Julie. Even when we were kids."

"My name is Ida. I always wanted to be an Elizabeth."

"Your daughter noticed the newspaper on the couch, didn't she? And Miss Carlyle's plate."

"She also noticed you, years ago, crossing the street at night to visit your friend Jane."

She nodded, staring down at the grass. "I tried to fool myself into believing the reason your daughter came was that you really were interested in antique glass. But I guess I knew all along. God, after all these years." Her voice was thick with tears. "Who'd think some youngster would pay attention to the comings and goings of people she hardly knew."

"She used to sit on the porch evenings. She couldn't help seeing you." I dug into my handbag and handed her some tissues. "She wasn't spying."

"And she remembers, she remembers—"

"She wouldn't have except for some prints she'd saved."

"I've heard. Oh, how I've heard. My daughter, the photographer." Wearily, she got to her feet. "Jane told me on the phone weeks ago she thought your daughter must be the one who babysat for us, the one who was always taking pictures. And do you know what I said?" she asked bitterly. "I said, 'Don't worry, you'll never run into her, and even if you did she wouldn't remember you. She was just a kid.'"

I looked toward the back of the yard. There was a rose arbor, and a white mesh-topped table with a yellow umbrella and four yellow-cushioned chairs. "Can't we sit there?"

Mrs. Tully mopped her face as we walked back, and

blew her nose. I put my handbag and the white envelope on the table.

After we sat down I waited for her to say something. She didn't. A single tear rolled down her cheek; she blotted it. I watched as she stared down at the sodden bunch of tissues in her square tanned hand. She turned them, clenched them; kept turning them, clenching them. I wanted to take them away from her.

I couldn't stand it any longer. "Mrs. Tully, nobody wants to hurt you. Nobody wants to ruin your life. Please trust me, please trust Chief Henderson."

For a moment she kept up the turning and clenching. Then: "What else can I do?" She threw the ball of tissues to the ground. For the first time in many minutes, she looked at me. "I've been in love with my husband since I was eight years old."

I nodded. "He played football."

"He was a quarterback in high school, and small as I was I never missed a game." She drew a deep unsteady breath. "When he got married, I cried. When the announcement of his son's birth appeared in the newspaper, I cried again. My parents called it a schoolgirl crush; they said I'd laugh about it someday. But God forgive me, I didn't feel like laughing until his wife died. My parents got impatient, short with me. A parent myself now, I realize they must have been frightened."

"Why? You had nothing to do with it."

"I mean frightened for me, that I still cared that much. Years had passed."

"What happened to your husband's first wife? What made her die?"

"Something inside. Liver or kidney, one of those." She looked away. "I'm so full of guilt I wish I could throw up and get it all out of me. She was so young."

"You were younger."

"Yes, but don't you see? I was glad." She sighed. "He was on the road a lot. I knew his mother, she was my Sunday school teacher, and I used to stop in to see her, and the baby."

"How old were you then?"

"Almost seventeen. Eighteen, when my husband and I started dating. Not often."

"But that was the beginning." I smiled, hoping she'd relax a little.

"No, not for a long time. Usually he took out older girls. I was so jealous." She shook her head. "But I grew up, and I got older too."

I hesitated, then I said it: "And pregnant."

"That's what I told him."

The back door was thrust open. "Mom?"

"Yes? What now?"

"Could we have a chocolate chip too?"

Slight hesitation. "One apiece, and that's all."

"Thanks, Mom."

I waved a bug away. "So you needed a baby."

"That's the way it was. I'd planned to pretend a miscarriage when he was away on business unless I conceived real soon." She lifted her shoulders. "I couldn't make it, then or ever. But Jane was expecting again."

"You two never lost touch, did you?"

She shook her head. "Her baby was promised, it was on

order, but the client got pregnant herself. Jane could have found another market, but she let me have her."

"Did you pay for the baby?"

"Only living expenses and the hospital. She'd kept the down payment from the other buyer. She and Benny almost broke up over me, but she knew all I had was my father's insurance money. It wasn't like with the doctor, that first time."

"What doctor?"

"What does it matter? He was old; he's dead now. He knew a couple who wanted a child. They gave her eight thousand dollars. She had to promise never to tell anyone about the baby, and to move away."

"Did she tell you that?"

"She told me everything those first few years. It seemed almost like bragging. She said it was easy to market babies, that some people would pay almost anything. But after a while she got more professional."

"Professional? How? Contracts?"

"Not written ones," Mrs. Tully said, "but she had ways of managing her own insurance. I've often thought that first baby was where she got her business education. And in her way, she was ethical."

"In what way, ethical?"

"She never named names. Not even to me, later. She insisted on living close to the people the baby was contracted to while it was baking. A constant reminder to her clients of an unwritten agreement, I suppose, but a way of checking on them, too. She was careful who she dealt with. She stuck to her price, whatever it was, and she quietly left town right after the transaction was completed. No more communication."

"That must have been a great relief to the new parents. A big selling point right there."

"It was part of the bargain. And she took excellent care of the babies from the moment they were started."

I thought of Julie's refrigerator, the prenatal pills, the fruit and skim milk, and the sun baths, and the scheduled swims, and the abstinence from alcohol and tobacco. How carefully she had prepared her product for market.

I said, "Do you know who the natural father of your daughter is?"

"Why should I care? She's who she is, isn't she? Smart, good girl, healthy. I imagine it was Benny. That's how they started out, he and Jane."

"Was he always the father?"

"Most of the time. Sometimes they used artificial insemination for family resemblance, if that's what the buyer wanted. Benny knew about those things from his lab and hospital work."

"What did you do about a birth certificate?"

"Benny took care of it. He could get anything from passports to Social Security cards."

"Did he deliver babies too?"

Mrs. Tully shook her head. "He was always there, but Jane didn't need him. She told me once that having a baby for her was like any other woman going to the bathroom. Maybe because she kept in practice, I don't know. She said every baby had been perfect."

I wondered what would have happened if one of those babies had not been "perfect."

"Mrs. Tully, do you have any idea who might have killed your friend? Anyone who might have had a reason?"

"No."

"We haven't talked about that part at all. Aren't you upset, or angry or sad? That someone killed her?"

She turned on me then. "What in hell do you think I'm sitting here with you for? Not only my whole life going down the drain, but no Jane. Jane is gone. I can't talk to her ever again."

I'd gone too far. I reached over for my handbag. I wouldn't have liked me either.

"No, wait a minute." The tanned square hand clamped tight on my wrist.

I waited.

"I think it really hasn't hit me yet. I haven't faced it yet." She let go of my wrist and leaned down for a long blade of grass crowding the table leg. She straightened and began tearing it into strips. "I loved her. When I saw it in the paper, I kept reading it over and over. I didn't believe it. She always called herself Julie, and I knew where she was living, but I didn't know what last name she was using, or who Benny was supposed to be this time. I tried to think, or hope, that it was just a coincidence, the town. I couldn't believe it was Jane."

"Do you now?"

She nodded. "Now, I do." She looked at me, her eyes red-rimmed. "I couldn't have stopped her, you know. Doing what she was doing."

"No."

"Another layer of guilt though."

"You're carrying a pretty heavy load as it is."

"That's what I keep telling myself. Funny." She turned her attention again to the blade of grass in her hands. "Jane wasn't much of a student. She wasn't much of anything. She never tried; she never cared. It wasn't until she went into big business making babies that she began to take pride in her work."

18

I was up at six, tiptoeing around, not wanting to wake Ellen and the twins. At six-thirty, after juice and cereal, I was on my way. As I was waiting to make the turn onto Route 80, a blue Corvette zoomed to a stop beside me. A blond teenager was driving, a racked tennis racket on the seat beside her. She smiled up at me, then pulled away with a roar. Beautiful teeth. In a way, she reminded me of a very young Julie.

I wondered if I could be turning paranoid. Would I, for the rest of my life, every time I saw a blond, blue-eyed young thing, imagine she might be one of Julie Gordon's carefully manufactured products?

Route 80 was pleasant; the sun was bright. I took my sunglasses from the dash. A few cars passed, tarpaulins flapping. Every summer, it seemed, there were more travel trailers on the road than last.

Young families in rumpled clothing were pulling into the rest areas, lugging coolers, starting breakfast at redwood tables.

It was getting warm. I pressed the button, closing the windows, and switched on the air-conditioner.

Julie Gordon must have made many people happy through the years, providing them with children. If she never named names, not even to her close and only friend, why would anyone want to kill her?

Or did she have a sideline along with the work in which she'd taken so much pride?

It had to be Benny, the man they'd called Harlon Pierce in the newspapers, and Julie Gordon I'd heard talking in the solarium at the Brock party. Because who else with such thick gray hair—obviously the wig I'd seen in the closet—had been there that night? Who else but Julie–Jane would have been walking alone up the driveway to a side door when any other guest would be making a grand entrance at the front?

"You're getting greedy, babe," Benny had said, "greedy, greedy, greedy."

But Julie hadn't always been greedy. Not with Mildred Tully.

Or that's what Mildred Tully told me. But what had Miss Carlyle, one of her teachers, told me about Mildred Tully? Born actress, Miss Carlyle had said.

The silver-gray car behind me, tailgating, started to pull out as if to pass, then dropped back. I looked at my speedometer. Fifty-five.

The night of the Brock party I'd thought I was listening in on the break-up of a marriage, the bitter talk of the bitter end: money.

Alimony? Blackmail? What else?

How many children could Julie, from age sixteen to age thirty-two or so, have produced so perfectly? One every year? One every two years?

Thousands of dollars, the first time around. Where had she gone from there? Who were her clients? There must have been many. And many stories to go with them.

I would tell Chief Henderson the little I knew in case

he didn't already know. Which probably he did. But maybe he didn't.

A headache was lurking.

That silver-gray car was still behind me.

Penny Wilde was heading for her bike when I pulled in the parking lot at market. Carrying a basket, she came over to the car. "Hi, Ida. Don't you ever stay home anymore?"

"I'm home most of the time."

"Not lately. I was over at your place the minute I heard about the fire yesterday. You weren't there. I was sure you'd hurry back, but when I called last night"—she lifted her shoulders—"nobody home. And this morning—"

"I just got back."

"Well, yeah; obviously." She laughed. "Where'd you go this time?"

"Ellen's."

"Again? Is everything all right there?"

"Fine; dandy. Why?"

"Just wondered. Usually you don't go buzzing off so frequently for such short stays. I thought maybe you'd gone to the Poconos."

"What for?"

"To see the new Brock baby. Nobody's seen him yet, including Mrs. Brock."

"I thought she was driving up the day before yesterday."

"She didn't go. Every day she gets a call, telling her not to come, that they're bringing the baby down that afternoon. Then something happens and they don't show. We thought maybe she'd asked you to go there as an emissary or spy or something."

"No. Who's the we who thought that?"

"Oh, Mrs. Smith and Margaret and—" She looked vague. "I forget who else." She brightened. "Look." She slid the handle of the basket off her wrist, and turned back an umbrella-like covering of tissue paper. Inside was a tiny gray kitten with round gray eyes. "Darling?"

"Darling. What happened to the old kitten?"

"He was antisocial; scratched me all the time—even after I stopped taking him for bike rides. I gave him to the S.P.C.A. They gave me this one." Penny stroked the little body, then pulled the tissue paper back in place. "What do you say to a cookout tomorrow night?"

"I'll check with Walt and call you this evening."

On my way to Fresh Produce, I thought of Penny Wilde and Joe and their children. All three kids had beautiful teeth, blond hair, and bright blue eyes.

Out in the parking lot I saw another silver-gray car. I hadn't realized that color was so popular this year.

My headache had arrived.

19

The outside of our double garage door was painted white. Now my side of it was drifted with gray. I left my car in the driveway and went into the house through the front door. Someone had sprayed the rooms with pine-scented freshener, but there still was the lingering smell of smoke. In the kitchen, the door that led down into the garage had two strips of wood nailed across it. The knob was gone.

Carrying the overnight bag, I went upstairs and took two aspirins. I made the bed, and put Walt's shirt and socks in the hamper. Then I went downstairs and back outside.

There was an unfamiliar maroon sedan parked across the street in front of the widow's house, the man in the driver's seat scribbling in a ledger propped up on the wheel. An inspector of some kind, I thought, or one of the local community tax men.

When I rolled up the garage door, the stench of dead fire hit me. I looked at the charred wall, the smoke-blackened door to the kitchen, the black-blistered remains of the stairs that had led to it. On the right, Walt's side, all was neat and clean: the power mower in its corner, the pegboard above it holding gardening tools. Farther down, toward the door, there was the red gasoline can with its capped spout, and the little wagon of bagged mulch, and the narrow shelf Walt had mounted high for weed killer and bug sprays.

The maroon sedan across the street, after a few false starts, drove away with a roar. Half a minute later, Chief Henderson pulled his official car into the driveway next to mine.

He sauntered into the garage. "You made good time," he said amiably.

How did he know? "No better than usual. I left early."

Hands in his pockets, he looked around. "It could have been worse," he said.

"The whole house could have gone." I gestured toward the blackened wall, what was left of the steps. "The fire was set right there."

"Set?"

"Certainly, set. There was no way a fire could have started by itself under those stairs. No wiring there, no oil-soaked cloths, no papers, no combustibles of any kind. I know the rules. Somebody tried to burn our house down."

"Do you have any idea why?"

"No."

"Ida, is there any reason anyone might want to harm you?"

"I wasn't even here."

"The arsonist might not have known that."

"Even if the arsonist didn't, he wouldn't have tried to start a killing fire in the middle of the day. I would have been alert then, would have heard something or smelled the smoke."

"What's over the garage here? Your bedroom?"

"No, the den. We've been sleeping downstairs in the family room the past couple of weeks."

"Yeah, the heat. We have too. What's up in the den?"

"A desk, books, a couple of reading chairs. You've been in there." Then: "It must have been that prowler."

He shook his head. "I don't think so, Ida."

"Why not?"

"The stranger seen in this neighborhood the night of the Brock party sounded very much like Benny Quick."

"Who saw him?"

"One of your neighbors down the street. Driving by."

"Benny was working the party."

"Not for long. He was gone when you left, remember?"

"It couldn't have been. He died that weekend. I've told you, somebody's been in this house several times since. I just know it."

"Then we have two different intruders, don't we?"

That hadn't occurred to me. "But there's nothing here. No money, no—" I looked at him. "What else?"

Again he shook his head. "Something somebody needs? Something you got here that can't be found? So what the hell, let's burn the whole thing up?" He kept shaking his head. "I don't know."

He looked discouraged, tired. I felt sorry for him.

"Well, you have more important things to think about right now," I said. "Walt says you're looking into that New York bank account Julie—"

"Yeah. It'll be in the papers tonight."

"Tell me now."

"Two hundred thousand dollars in cash was deposited

in Julie Gordon's name in that bank over a year ago. The money was clean, and the account wasn't used until about a week before Gordon moved here."

"Who made the deposit?"

"A Mr. Gordon."

"Benny Quick."

"I wouldn't be surprised. Seems they had a lot of money to play with, those two."

"Did you find out where he went when he took the car all those nights?"

"He wasn't catering, that's for sure. Just drove, from what we've learned so far. Out in the foothills, or up on the mountains." Chief Henderson was talking, but he was thinking about something else. His eyes kept going to the charred ceiling over the stairs. "He stopped at the spas and the country clubs, all the affluent places, claiming he was looking for somebody the members never heard of."

"That's an old one. But what for?"

He shrugged. "It's old, but it worked. Usually he'd end up drinking with some kindly soul who wanted to help him find his long-lost buddy, and before you knew it he was talking to people about themselves, their friends and neighbors, and the whole damn community."

Walt pulled in then behind my car. "I meant to be here when you got back. Didn't expect you so early."

"Otherwise the bed would have been made the minute you got up, right?"

"Right."

"There's no damage that can't be repaired, hon."

"No." He came in, gave me a quick hug and we stood

side by side, gazing at the blackened stairway. "What did you have stored under the stairs?"

"That pile of darkened glass you see there was a carton of canning jars I never got around to using. The metal was a jungle-gym Ellen asked us not to put up until next year."

"What was in the garbage can?" Chief Henderson asked.

I wondered how he could tell it once had been a garbage can. "Only a fresh liner. We use it when we're having people over for a cookout, for paper plates and things."

"That's where the fire was set," Walt said. "In that can."

Of course. I looked around the garage again. "Did the Scouts come around collecting paper any time when I was away?"

"Not that I know of."

"There was a stack of newspapers bound in twine over on your side, just inside the door."

"Yeah," Walt said, "so there was."

"Walt doesn't remember how much gasoline was here," Chief Henderson said.

I looked over at the squat, red three-gallon can on the garage floor. "Is it empty?"

"Just about."

"It shouldn't be. I had it filled Sunday morning. Neither of us has mowed the lawn since."

The Chief, leaning against the doorway, was rubbing his chin. "The fire wasn't planned, at least not for yesterday. The materials used were on hand, right here. Impulse. What triggered it?"

I thought of Mildred Tully and the hand cultivator. Impulse. What if she had been on her feet with a knife in her hand?

We turned and wandered out of the garage. Walt was going back to the office; Chief Henderson was going back to his. If all went well, they would meet at the club around five-thirty for a quick nine holes.

I was checking the mail as they pulled out. It was a bonanza—a letter from our daughter in Denver, a picture post card from our son backpacking in Arizona, and the new mystery I'd ordered from the book club.

"Hey, hon—" I turned. Walt had backed up in front of the house, had rolled his window down, and was leaning out. "Want to play a few with us? I could pick you up."

I shook my head, smiling, holding up my brown-wrapped book.

I never joined Walt and his golfing buddies unless it was a split foursome. One would think he'd have noticed that through the years.

Standing at the kitchen table, I read the mail, smiling a little. I cut the wrapper off the new book, took chops from the freezer, then went upstairs to change. Five minutes out of the shower, before I'd even donned the shorts and sleeveless blouse, I was feeling sticky again.

This was no day for chops. I put them back in the freezer, and picked up the new book on my way down to the family room.

It would be too hot to sit out and read on the patio, but I opened the sliding door for circulation. Walt had forgotten to lock it last night. I would bring this small matter to his attention. I switched on an FM program, low.

I wanted to tell him about Mildred Tully.

He won't be gone long.

Walt is a good husband. He lost a tournament by default in Buffalo years ago, and all because of false labor pains.

What's better than a brand-new book, never read by anyone before, the stiff way it opens, the smell of it; the clean, clear print?

How could he want to play golf when somebody tried to burn our house down?

This book is bound to be a grabber. You could hardly wait for it to come.

During the first few chapters, thoughts of the fire, the faceless person who set it, of the Tullys, of Julie Gordon, all kept intruding. Once, I paused long enough to switch on the tall lamp at my elbow. It wasn't yet six, but the sky had darkened. Thunder was rumbling in the distance. The soothing background music on the radio was punctuated with static. Lightning somewhere.

I put my book face down on the sofa and went upstairs to tear lettuce for a salad. I carved the avocado into chilled grapefruit sections. Walt would get off the course the minute he saw lightning.

There was a breeze now. It was following me up the stairs into the kitchen. Curtains began to stir. The temperature was dropping.

Maybe this time we really were in for rain. A storm, I hoped; a good one.

I went back to the freezer for the chops, and put them on the cupboard counter.

The phone rang, but when I reached it there was no one.

I went out to get the local paper. The stiffening breeze felt good.

There was a black car parked across the street, a little way down from the widow's house. I wondered if they were true, those stories I'd heard about the widow and a lover she joined every time she left for Canada with her poodles. If so, and who cared, who would be checking? Her husband was long gone. Or, maybe— Could the lover have a wife?

Or, how about the lover being very rich, and the relatives—preferably in-laws—having an eye on his money?

I had stopped expecting to see Julie Gordon's name in the papers, but I hadn't stopped looking for it. This early evening, on the back page of the first section, there were a few short lines: Julie Gordon's body had been claimed for burial by Mr. and Mrs. Roland Cowell of Bainbridge, New Jersey. I wondered if Roland was her brother or father.

Julie had a resting place now.

The thunder was overhead. The curtains were billowing. I lowered the windows, keeping them slightly open for the fresh breeze, and turned on the outside light for Walt. I left a lamp glowing dimly in the living room.

Downstairs, it was blessedly cool. I turned off the radio with its scratchy static, listened with pleasure to the thunder, reached for my book, and settled down under the pool of lamplight. My headache was gone.

Lightning was closer now; there were cracking sounds. I thought I heard Walt upstairs. "Hon?"

No answer. I went back to my book.

I had turned to Chapter XIII when the first pebbles hit the screen. "Penny?"

More pebbles. Or I thought they were pebbles. "Penny?"

I couldn't see out there. "Penny," I said sharply, "cut it out! Come on in!"

But Penny didn't come in. Uneasy, I put my book aside. The screen began to slide open. Silence between the claps of thunder. A man stepped over the sill, a big man.

"What do you want?"

The man half lifted his hand. Slowly, deliberately, he started toward me.

I twisted, scrambling out of the lamp's light. I ran for the stairs, pulling on the rail up to the darkness of the kitchen. At the top, I looked back over my shoulder. He stood down there at the foot of the stairs, legs spread, the light behind him. I couldn't see his face.

He said something, but I didn't hear it. Another crash of thunder. Then I saw the other two, coming through the screen.

Three against one!

Half turned, I reached back in the darkness, fumbling for a hold on the cupboard. One more step. The other two men, shadowy, were moving toward the stairs. My hand landed on the frozen chops. My fingers curled around the package. I hurled it down the stairs. Then I slammed the kitchen door and bolted it.

The kitchen light snapped on.

20

Again the storm went around us. There still was thunder but it was moving away; the sky directly above was brightening. On our way to the police station, we could see the grayness in the surrounding foothills. Over there somewhere they were getting the rain our own farmers needed so desperately.

The breeze had died down.

Those silver-gray cars are everywhere these days, I thought as we pulled into the municipal parking lot. Because here was another one.

The brick stairs leading up into the police station reminded me of the entrance to the hospital morgue.

"Is this man who he says he is?" Chief Henderson asked.

The man, sitting in one of the chairs in front of the desk, stood up as we entered the Chief's office.

"If he says his name is Tully," I said, "he is. He's Mildred Tully's husband."

"You know him well?"

"Not well. They live in Plains, where we used to live. Our daughter babysat for them."

"I didn't mean to frighten you," Mr. Tully said. "I heard you tell me to come in."

"I thought you were someone else, a neighbor. She throws pebbles against the screen sometimes."

"I didn't throw any pebbles, Mrs. Pelham. I saw you sitting in there so I knocked on the frame of the screen."

A young man I'd never seen before was standing near the open windows. He brought another chair and placed it before Chief Henderson's desk. The Chief waved a hand.

Mr. Tully, Walt, and I sat down. The young man went back to his place near the windows.

"If you had come to the front door," I said to Mr. Tully, "I would have heard you."

"I did. When you didn't answer, I looked for a back door. Your car was there; I assumed you were home somewhere. I walked around the fence, and saw you sitting in that room off the patio. I thought you might even be expecting me."

"Why?" Chief Henderson asked.

"My wife."

"Did she know you were following Mrs. Pelham?"

"Following? No. That sounds sinister. No, my wife would have started thinking this morning, mulling things over, blaming herself for God knows what. She would have found out I wasn't in New Haven where I'd said I'd be, and she would have put two and two together, and she would have telephoned Mrs. Pelham."

I remembered the phone ringing during the thunder and the lightning.

Sounds of cars out on the parking lot came through the open windows.

"I just wanted to talk with you," Mr. Tully said.

I looked at him. "Then why didn't you? When I was there at your house?"

"Because I didn't know how afraid Mildred was. Not until after you left. I didn't know what you'd come for. She told me late last night."

Mr. Tully seemed in complete control—if not of the situation, certainly of himself. Even when he'd said, "I didn't know what you'd come for," his tone hadn't hardened in suspicion or resentment.

He said, "Mildred told me she tried to injure you last night. She was upset because she'd come so close to it." He paused. "You were driving away when I got to your daughter's house this morning."

"Why didn't you stop me?"

"My wife thinks you're afraid of her now. If that's true, you'd hardly pull over with a friendly smile when you saw me."

I would have. "So you followed all the way?"

"I thought you'd be stopping for coffee, or breakfast; that I could talk with you then. You'd feel safe in a public place. But you drove straight through."

Walt lifted his head. Family rule: stop every two hours if only to stretch.

Chief Henderson, listening, had been watching the eraser of his pencil as he doodled in circles around and around on the top of his desk. He put the pencil down. "You wanted to talk with Mrs. Pelham." He looked at Tully. "Do you mind telling me why?"

"To ask her to leave my wife alone." Tully looked back at him, eyes level. "I know my wife didn't physically deliver our daughter. I've always known it, and I was pretty sure I knew where the baby came from. But it didn't matter because I knew why Mildred did what she did." His tone was even, matter-of-fact. "My wife didn't kill her friend Jane, or Julie Gordon, as you people call her, and I sure as hell didn't. We don't think we have any information you don't already have, but we'll help if we can. All we ask is that you keep out of our lives. No publicity. We don't want our children hurt."

"Nobody does," Chief Henderson said. "We've begun to look into possibilities of blackmail."

Mr. Tully shook his head. "Don't look in my wife's direction. She hasn't had any money of her own since her father died, and you know where that went."

The Chief nodded. "We won't keep you any longer, Mr. Tully. If you think of anything—"

There was a long moment of silence after Mr. Tully left. Chief Henderson was tapping the eraser of his pencil softly, rhythmically, on the desk. Then: "Ida, I understand there's a letter."

"Yes. I have it right here." I dug into my handbag. "I was going to tell you about it." I handed him the envelope.

He read the letter, then read it again. He picked up the envelope and looked at it, front and back. No comment.

Walt was looking at me. I wondered what Mrs. Tully had told Mr. Tully about me and that letter, and what Mr. Tully had told Chief Henderson.

I got up and went over to stand near the young man at the windows. Mr. Tully had crossed the parking lot and was opening the door of the silver-gray car. He glanced at his watch, then slid under the wheel.

Waves of disapproval emanated from the silence behind me. Well, yes, I thought, I should have called the

Chief immediately about the letter. Then I thought: but what's done is done. Or not done, as the case may be. I looked at the young man next to me. "I don't think we've ever met," I said pleasantly, "or even seen each other."

"I've seen you." He seemed amused.

"Are you the one who was in the car parked across the street?"

"I'm the one."

"I thought you were snooping on the widow."

"I'm a police officer," he said.

Why had I used that word, snoop? "You're not in uniform," I said, "but I should have known."

"Officer Barlow was keeping an eye on your house, Ida," Chief Henderson said. "He was the one who alerted us this afternoon, the same officer who reported the fire in your garage."

"Thank you, officer."

"Lucky timing, Mrs. Pelham. I wasn't stationed out there full time like today. I was on patrol, driving by; the smoke was curling out from under the door."

"If you were stationed out front today, then you must have seen him. Was Mr. Tully telling the truth? Did he come to the front door first."

"Yes."

"I didn't hear him."

"It was thundering then. I thought you might not, depending on where you were in the house. I didn't call headquarters until I saw him go around the back."

A nice young man; brown hair, brown eyes. Dedicated. Sincere. He would go far. Chief Henderson could always spot the good ones.

When the young man left the office, I told Chief Henderson that.

"Um-hmm."

I sat down again.

The Chief leaned farther back in his chair. "Ida, what happened at the Tully house last evening?"

"I didn't mean to make her cry," I said. Then I told him, everything, almost word for word. "Julie Gordon conceived and sold babies to order," I finished. "Mrs. Tully knew it."

"Did Mrs. Tully say whether or not Julie was still working through the doctor?" he asked. "The one who placed her first baby?"

"She said he died. I got the impression the unwritten contracts were private arrangements."

"Did she tell you how these unwritten contracts came about?" Walt asked. "Who the contacts were?"

I shook my head. "No."

"Any number of ways," Chief Henderson said. "The word gets around in operations like this. And Benny Quick obviously had connections somewhere, although I suspect he made some of his own. He had something on his mind when he was doing all that country-clubbing."

"Fishing for future prospects," I said.

"Could be."

Walt's stomach was grumbling. I stood up. "Was that envelope in Julie's mailbox anything?"

The Chief nodded. "Addressed to J. Gordon. Two one-way airline tickets to Memphis out of Harrisburg."

"For when?" Walt asked.

"A four o'clock flight on Monday, the day after they were killed."

"They would have been leaving the same way they came," Walt said, getting to his feet, "probably even to unloading the car before flight time."

"And changing names and planes in Memphis," Chief Henderson said.

I had turned to leave. I turned back. "It was perfectly timed, wasn't it? Baby arrives sometime Saturday night. Early Sunday morning baby is delivered to buyer. Fee is collected and Julie heads back to— Fee! Mrs. Tully said she got thousands for a baby!"

Again the Chief nodded. "And only seventy bucks in her wallet."

On the way home, I said, "If you killed someone for thousands of dollars, you wouldn't bother with any small change that might be in a wallet, would you?"

"Nope. The idea," Walt said, "would be to get out of there as fast as possible."

"Somebody else must have bought those plane tickets. If it had been Julie or that man Quick, they wouldn't have had them mailed. So somebody knew Julie would be free to travel on Monday."

"Sounds like it."

"Somebody she was in close touch with. Maybe even the one who ordered the baby. As soon as she goes into labor the tickets are bought and paid for." It was almost nine, and the sun was low and red in the sky. "You didn't play golf today, did you? You never really planned to."

"We could see there'd be a storm."

"Not that early you couldn't."

"Weather forecast."

"We've been going through those weather forecasts for ages now," I said mildly. "Nobody around here believes in weather forecasts anymore. Know what I think?"

"What?"

"I think you and the Chief made that big to-do out in front of the house about your golf game because you wanted somebody else to hear. You wanted somebody to think I'd be alone."

He didn't say anything.

"I bet Officer Barlow saw Tully's car pull up and park down the block, maybe even suspected he'd been following me when he saw the New Jersey plates. That was no accident, you and two policemen being there when Tully finally showed at the house, the men outside and you in the kitchen."

He didn't deny it. I didn't know whether it was because he couldn't deny it, or just didn't want to argue. He turned in the driveway and parked his car next to mine. The lights I had turned on for him when the storm was threatening were still burning.

Out in the kitchen, I said, "What do you want to eat?"

"What have you got?"

The door down into the family room was open. No one had turned off the lamp. "The chops should be defrosted by now." I started down the stairs.

"They aren't down there," Walt said. "You bopped one of the cops. I gave them to him."

"Good. The least we could do."

"Ida, I said—"

"I heard you. Be right back."

I switched on the patio lights, slid the door open, and stepped out. The crickets were raucous; probably thirsty. So were my plants.

There were no pebbles on the patio floor. Mr. Tully had told the truth. Whenever Penny tossed pebbles against the screen, I always found the clutter later.

"The package was intact, hon," Walt said as I came back up the stairs. "It was still partially frozen."

"Did you think I was down there on my hands and knees looking for a stray chop?" I chuckled. "I was just checking the patio, turning out lights." I closed the door at the top of the stairs. "Walt, what if Mr. Tully hadn't followed me home to talk about his wife? What if he was after that letter?"

"It sounded as if he'd been pretty candid about it to Henderson." Walt was standing at the open refrigerator, peering in. "Up to then, Henderson didn't know anything about it. Neither did I."

"Tully didn't know that. And don't forget, he wasn't in the police station voluntarily. He sat in his car right down this street thinking about something pretty seriously for a long time."

"Yeah. He did, didn't he? I don't know. Beats me."

"What if Mrs. Tully hadn't written it?" I asked. "What if she knew who did?"

Walt had a question of his own. "How about a ham and cheese on rye?" he said.

21

The road to Chill Lake was black-topped, winding, and narrow. High old trees crowded close. One, toppled years ago by a storm or old age, lay alongside like a stricken giant, an ivied playground now for two frolicsome squirrels.

At home the heat had closed in again, but soon after I'd turned off Route 80 I switched off the air-conditioner. Here in the Poconos it was cool, quiet, fragrant. There were no other cars.

Sleep hadn't come any easier last night than the night before. I'd finished the new book but just as I was drifting into sleep I remembered Penny Wilde's words at market. Eleanor Brock hadn't yet seen her grandson.

Why? A way to make her yearn for the child even more? A way of punishing her for something?

What if there was no baby?

A fleeting thought. Outrageous. Ridiculous.

By noon I couldn't stand it any longer. I'd left a note for Walt on the kitchen table, remembered to pick up the new book, and started the two-hour drive to the mountains.

Howie Brock was carrying an overnight case to his car in the long dirt driveway as I pulled in. He threw it in the back seat. I began to back up.

"Halt," Howie called, laughing, holding up his hand. "Stay where you are. I'll go around you."

He came over to the car, looking as if he'd just come from the shower, smelling of aftershave. His hair, wavy and golden, must have been blown dry. "I'm going down to see if the apartment is as bad as Ma says it is."

"Bad? How?"

"Ma says it's too hot. She wants us to bring the baby to the house and stay for a few weeks. Linda wants to go straight to the apartment. Natch."

"Is the apartment too hot?"

"Shouldn't be. It's air-conditioned. Ma knows it; she just didn't turn the knob. You know Ma. She's made up her mind the apartment is hot, so it's hot." He sighed. "You see standing before you a man torn between two women. No." He nodded back toward the cabin. "Make that three."

"You aren't the first, and you won't be the last."

Pearl, his mother-in-law, appeared on the porch, her blue paisley caftan swaying in the slight breeze.

Howie started back to his car, and I got out of mine.

"Ida, dear! What a lovely surprise! You're just in time for a very late lunch—"

"Oh, no, thanks, I just stopped by to—"

"We're on a completely different schedule now; time literally has turned around. Wait until you see our little angel." Then, as Howie started backing his car around mine: "Be careful with your driving, dear."

Howie tapped the horn as he pulled away. I reached in for my handbag and the book on the front seat.

Starting up the driveway under the trees I smiled apologetically at the woman on the porch. "I won't stay. I know how hectic it is, the first few days with a new baby." I bent automatically to pick up a couple of check-out counter slips. "Is he asleep?"

"Yes, but it doesn't matter. He's just been fed. He's good for another four hours." Pearl came to the top of the stairs as I started up them. "Did Eleanor Brock send you?" she asked.

"No, I was in the area. I got a new mystery yesterday, and I finished it last night. I thought Linda would like it."

"How thoughtful." She opened the screen door wide.

Pearl was always pleasant enough, but I suspected she had no great fondness for me. I was a friend of Eleanor Brock.

Linda was asleep on the sofa, half-turned on her side, one of her mother's cats curled at her feet.

"He's in here." Pearl, wafting her caftan and a musky scent, led me directly to a dim room at the back of the cabin. It smelled of baby powder. "Isn't he beautiful?"

The baby was sleeping on his stomach, lying very still, as new babies do, in an oval white-painted wicker basket. The basket was on a library table, near a screened tree-shaded window, and it was decorated with tiny hand-painted forget-me-nots. Pearl's handiwork, I supposed.

"Yes," I said. "Beautiful."

"They waited long enough for him, but he was worth waiting for. And so good." She moved an empty bottle from the corner of the table over to a utility tray next to a blue and white box of disposable diapers, then reached into the basket. Ever so gently she turned the sleeping baby, and lifted him, his fluffy blond head cupped in one square brown hand, his tiny diapered bottom cupped in the other. "He looks just like his father, doesn't he?"

Not exactly. Right now he looked more like his great-grandfather without the mustache. But the long, thin, curling Brock mouth was there; the flat elfin ears. "He's his father's son all right," I said. "He's so husky-looking. Why did he need an incubator?"

"He didn't." She was surprised. "Who told you that?"

"I don't know. Guess I got the wrong baby. So many new ones lately, I get them mixed up."

I would have liked to ask where the baby was born, but decided not to. The Chief could check the local hospital easily enough, if he hadn't already. Walt said he was checking new babies everywhere.

Tenderly she returned her grandson to his stomach in the basket, placing round arms at right angles, dimpled hands palms down. "Hard to believe he'll tower over us someday." She touched the square little back. "Let's have some sherry, shall we? You go in and sit down. I'll bring it."

I went back to the other room, pausing to look at the sketches and bold contemporary oils that covered the walls.

Linda was still sleeping. So was the cat. Pearl couldn't have too many mice around; not with her cats.

Hands in my pockets I wandered to the front of the cabin and stood looking out the front door. The trees, mostly pines, were high and old, patches of moss around the bases of them. The grass was sparse. There was a crumpled paper cup, and an abandoned golf ball out

there. Across the driveway a faded hammock was slung
between two white birches.

I could hear Pearl in the kitchen, humming, getting out
glasses, opening things.

My fingers were curled around the paper in my left
pocket. Suddenly aware of it, I remembered the scraps I'd
automatically picked up from the edge of the driveway. I
turned to look for a wastebasket, then I stopped. I
straightened them out. They were strips of paper, about
an inch wide, about eight inches long. They had four
black lines across them. One, gray, was printed: $1000.
The other, white, was marked: $2000. Both strips read in
small print at one end: Dry Seal, Coin Counter Co., Made
in U.S.A.

I slipped the strips back in my pocket.

"You'll like this," Pearl said, coming in with a tray. "A
friend brought it back from Paris. Eleanor wouldn't appreciate it of course; the only time she's ever been in Paris
was on one of those ghastly tours."

Ensconced in wicker rocking chairs at the other end of
the room we had sherry and nibbled on petits fours. Pearl
fitted a cigarette into an ebony holder, bracelets jingling.
The only ring she wore these days was her black pearl.
"Given to me by a poor unfortunate in the throes of early
love. At the inevitable end, I, of course, refused to return
it."

This had maddened Eleanor Brock. *That woman said
exactly that in the presence of all those people! My
friends!*

I'd heard about that two years ago.

And this cabin, according to Pearl, had been acquired

in the same manner. It, too, remained happily unrelinquished.

Pearl looked down the room at her sleeping daughter. "Poor Linda. She's so wonderfully happy, and so terribly tired."

"The two A.M. feeding won't be necessary for long if she plays her cards right. You said he was a good baby."

"Yes, but it isn't as easy to become a new mother at thirty as it is at twenty. I went through it myself, and once was enough. Linda's never really been strong. I wish she and the baby could stay on here with me for a few weeks. But Linda's afraid her mother-in-law would object. Do you think she would?"

I knew she would. "Probably," I said.

"But here, Linda would have me to help her. Eleanor Brock wouldn't. Oh, she'd moon over the kid, show him off to her friends, and boast about the presents she bought him, just the way she does with her granddaughters, but she wouldn't lift a finger if it meant one second of inconvenience."

"She's good to the kids, Pearl."

"Only when it pleases her."

"Why don't you ask her to lunch, let her see how good it is for the baby here, so cool and quiet."

Pearl shook her head. "It wouldn't work. And no matter what I say, my daughter thinks she has to please her mother-in-law. She wants her baby to get every bit as much from the Brocks as the other grandchildren get."

Linda stirred on the sofa. Her eyes were closed, but I wondered how long she had been awake. It could have been a long time.

Pearl must have had the same thought. "Let's face it," she said briskly, "Eleanor Brock doesn't approve of me, my housekeeping, or my lifestyle."

"So you're different. You're an artist, and you don't play golf."

"Having discarded four husbands along the way hasn't helped much either," Pearl said dryly.

"No, I suppose not."

I looked around at the piles of magazines, the canvases in a corner leaning against the wall. Pearl wasn't the disgraceful housekeeper Eleanor Brock said she was. This was clutter; not dirt.

"With my history, Eleanor thought it would be the same with Linda. But it was a love match, and Linda's first marriage," Pearl said significantly, "and she's still married. So all Eleanor Brock's hopes have been in vain."

Enough for today. I stood up, glass in hand. "I must go. Here, I'll help carry to the kitchen."

"No, no, just put it down. I wouldn't want even you to see that mess out there." She came with me to the door, switching on a lamp as she passed. "Tell Eleanor I've been delighted, having the baby here."

"Yes. Thanks for everything, Pearl. The book is on the wicker table."

"I see it. Is that thunder?"

"It doesn't mean anything." The sky was dark. "We've been going through this for weeks."

"We had a storm yesterday, but it didn't last long enough to do much good. The forests are dry."

"Here's hoping then. In any case, I'll be out of the mountains before it hits. If it does."

Pearl turned away, and as I started down the porch stairs her phone rang. I paused. I hadn't seen a phone, so probably it was in the kitchen. Would it be Walt for some reason? But there were only two rings, and after a minute I went on to my car.

As I started the engine, I touched the papers in my left pocket. They weren't check-out slips or candy wrappers, as I'd thought when I picked them up. But I'd seen strips of paper like these before.

And Pearl wasn't busy on the phone, either. As I pulled out, I could see her in the light of the lamp standing there behind the screen door.

22

The sky was growing darker. I lifted my wrist, but my watch wasn't there. It was home on the catch-all table near the shower in the upstairs bathroom. The clock on the dash said six. I didn't trust that clock; I never had.

I switched on the radio. There was something out there somewhere behind the static, but no good to me. I snapped it off.

Those strips of paper in my left pocket were straps. Banks put bills of the same denomination in straps. Different colors for different denominations. In my left pocket there were two of those straps; one for a thousand, one for two.

Not taking my eyes from the road, I reached into my left pocket. I came up with the gray one, the $1000 one, and held it atop the wheel. It looked fresh and crisp. The unmarked side had a dull sheen to it. I pressed one end of it over the other, making a ring. It held. Taking them apart, the ends came away easily enough. The same with the white one, but I saw now that the white one had been torn at one end.

So these were used straps.

Who worked for a bank? Not Pearl; not Howie; not Linda. Who, among Pearl's friends, visiting at the cabin, worked at a bank?

I didn't know of any. *That doesn't mean none exists.* Right.

But did bank people walk around with money straps in their pockets?

No, not unless they were strapped around money.

These had fallen from a car, or a handbag, or a pocket.

Thinking back, there had been a crumpled cigarette package farther down along the driveway too. Pearl, unless she happened to be out there, out of her dream world and observant at the time, never would have thought to pick anything up.

Thousands for a baby, Mildred Tully had said.

Anyone who knew about Julie's current consignment would have known about those thousands.

Somebody had packets of money from somewhere, from someone.

I visualized that shadowy somebody in a car, or under a tree in the country, or in a room somewhere, alone, slipping packets of bills out of straps marked $1000, $2000, maybe $5000. Counting, counting. And feeling so sure, so safe. Careless.

Why sure? Why safe? Why careless?

These straps were here in the mountains. They weren't up on the ridge where Julie died. Only her opened shoulder bag had been found there.

Could a somebody else have been at Pearl's cabin, in another room, when I was there? Pearl always had a male "somebody" of her own. And she hadn't wanted me in the kitchen this time.

All this may have absolutely nothing to do with Julie Gordon.

Right.

Lightning was slashing the sky. I slipped the straps back into my left pocket, remembering that one of the safest places in an electrical storm is a car. I also remembered that taking shelter under trees is not recommended. Did cars nullify trees?

I pressed the button to close the windows. A lone car coming toward me had lights on. I switched on mine.

In my rear view I could see the other car's brake lights. The driver must have decided to turn back.

I passed the cabin we used to rent when the children were little. It looked empty. The owners, I'd been told, had died in happy old age.

I hoped so, the happy old age part.

Lightning was closer, bright jagged flashes.

A car came up close behind me. I slowed, waiting for it to pass. It stuck with me.

The rain came. First a few tentative heavy plops on the hood and roof, and then the deluge. The windshield wipers went frantically, whipping back and forth, back and forth, the job undone a split-second later.

The car behind was very close, its lights disconcerting. I tilted the mirror away. That driver can't night-drive, I thought; I fought back my annoyance. I remembered the time in Buffalo I'd followed a bright red car in a blizzard. But at least I had dimmed my lights.

The rain shifted, pounding even harder against the car in its fury. It seemed almost personal, that fury. The lightning was all around, slashing, cracking.

The wet road shone blindingly under the headlights.

I wasn't afraid. I knew the road, didn't I? I'd driven it

hundreds of times. In another ten minutes, I'd be out of this.

The car behind me started to pass. I pulled over a little; not far. There was a ravine down there, big trees.

Only the car from behind didn't pass. It stayed with me. Side by side. It knocked against me, one time, two times, nudging me over.

"Hey, you—" I turned my head, furious.

Lightning flashed again. A brief, instant floodlight. My heart jumped. That wasn't a timid confused driver behind the wheel in the car next to me.

I stepped hard on the pedal. No good. Too late. He got me. There was the crunch of metal, the sickening slow slide down off the road, the jarring jolt as my car hit sideways against a tree.

The lid of the trunk popped open.

The other car slid ahead of me, and skidded around, ending with its nose pointing down into the ravine.

I scrambled across the seat. The door wouldn't open. The thick trunk of the tree was there.

This is how it was with Julie. She tried to get away too.

The windshield wipers still were swiping, the motor was running, the rain was drumming down. There was movement in the car in front of me.

Fear. The only thing to fear is . . .

I lay down on the seat, straightened and rolled up and over the back of it. On the floor of the rear I groped for the door handle. Oh, door, don't be jammed! Please, *please.*

It opened.

Howie was standing at the front of my car, on the edge

of the headlights' misty glare. "You're not going anywhere, Ida," he shouted. He had a gun in his hand.

In the next streak of lightning, his hair looked golden. Not even wet. The roaring, deafening crack didn't make him turn. For an instant I was blinded. "Get back in your car, Ida."

He kept shouting other things, but I don't remember what. The tree, reluctant, seemed to take so long to fall. It was graceful, a huge thing, a dark thing, groaning. Down, down, down, it came.

"Howie!"

He laughed. Then he turned. Then he screamed.

The tree crashed on Howie and his car. They all got mixed up together.

The rain came down, hard and cold. It was very dark. It must be nighttime, I thought.

23

I remember huddling down against the back right tire of my car. It wasn't so cold, so rainy, there, or I thought it wasn't. I remember thinking I ought to get into the back seat while I was figuring out what to do.

The giant pine had fallen diagonally across the road, tilting and pushing Howie's car farther down into the ravine. It had dragged mine halfway around the stout trunk of an old maple. Incongruously, the headlights still were glowing. The motor ticked.

"Ida!" It was a shout.

I lifted my head.

"Ida, Ida, Ida, Ida—" Each shout louder than the last. I'd thought he was dead.

"I can see you, Ida. I know where you are."

How could he?

Chains of lightning flashed. Yes. That's how he could see where I was.

"Get up, Ida. This gun is pointed straight at you. Come down here."

I pulled myself up. Holding on, I started moving around the maple to the front of the car.

"Get me out of here, Ida." He was under a pile that would take a bulldozer. In the lights of my car it was a cavernous mountain. Looking out at me, up at me, right hand free, Howie had the gun. "Ida, do something! I'm bleeding all over the place."

I pushed back sopping hair. Had he really tried to kill me? "I don't know what to do. I have to get help."

"There's a jack in the trunk of your car."

"No—"

"Don't lie," he shouted. "I saw it when I took the gasoline can out. Get it!"

"I have to have my keys." If I could get around to the other side of the car—

"The hell you do! The trunk's sprung, and you know it! Now get moving!"

"I can't turn my back. You'll shoot me."

"Not while I need you." Thunder crashed. "That's your guarantee. But if you try anything—"

"I know, I know." I screamed it through the rain and the thunder. "What a waste of time you've been to everybody."

I stumbled my way back around the maple to the trunk of the car, sensing the gun on my back.

There was no way. Maybe I would have made a try for it if I'd thought I'd be killed outright. If he got me. But maiming, or crippling, or a mind that doesn't work anymore— I was afraid.

Slipping and sliding, falling once on pine needles, I made it with the support of tree trunks all the way down the incline.

"I can't do it, Howie. It would take a crew of giants."

Even my teeth were aching from the cold.

"Put the jack there," Howie called. "Right where

you're standing. Just a couple of inches will get me out of here."

He was pale. His face was wet, but not from the rain. He was under the slanting curve of the fender.

It didn't work.

"The bumper's at an angle, Howie. The jack can't get a bite on it."

"You're not trying," Howie yelled. "You think if you leave me here long enough I'll bleed to death. Listen, Ida, when I start to fade, you're going with me!"

I tried again and again, always with the gun pointing at me. I tried not to turn my back completely. Spinal injuries sometimes can't be fixed. I kept thinking that. "I can't," I cried out, "I can't, I can't. Let me go. You're bleeding so bad, Howie, and I can't help you."

"Why should you?" He laughed. "You're cold, aren't you? All wet and cold. I'm warm. Good red blood around me. That's all good, blue, red blood, I'll have you know." He laughed again.

"You're hemorrhaging, Howie. Please put that gun down."

"Can't do that. Sorry. Don't want to kill you. You're just a nice lady turning nosey in your old age. Nothing else to do, am I kee-rect?"

Shivering, I thought longingly of steaming clam broth in a thick warm mug.

"Kee-rect?" Howie thrust the gun.

"Y-yes, right. Correct."

"Julie, now, she deserved it. I knew what she did, selling babies. But I never heard there was a follow-up, other installments, pay or we'll tell your mother on you."

A quick move, and out of the line of fire. That was the thing to do. "You have to have a doctor, Howie."

"Get back to that jack! Move it over an inch."

I moved it over. I tried again. I didn't own a bone that didn't ache. I wished miserably for home.

"The trouble with Julie," my murderer was shouting at me, "is that she didn't know when to stop. She knew how Ma was. She knew you'd tell Ma all about her."

"I didn't know about Julie."

"Keeper of the exchequer, that's Ma; guardian of our morals, president of the board. Emotional blackmailer, par excellence. Witness dear old Dad. If he'd kept his peccadilloes under wraps—but, oh, no."

"I can't do it, Howie. Not this way. The jack keeps slipping. Maybe if I tried from another angle?"

"No, you don't. Stay right where you are, where I can see you. You can do it if you want to. When we leave, we'll leave this place together."

He was dying. I could see the blood seeping out from under him. His nose had begun to bleed.

Yet he was still shouting. How could he do that?

How was it my car lights were still on? Why didn't they go out when the rest of the car did?

I couldn't tell Howie he was dying. He'd take me with him.

I moved the jack one more time and tried to pump.

"Ida, come here!"

My cold wet hands slipped off the jack handle. "Turn the gun away."

He turned it away, but he held onto it.

"Sit down," he said pleasantly. "Keep me company."

He'd said it the same way one sunny day years ago on the porch at the club. I sat down on sodden ground, half under the tilted fender, my teeth chattering. Howie's hand, the gun, were only inches away from me.

Clam broth. Hot, hot clam broth.

"Ida, it's all your fault," he said reproachfully. "You never liked Julie."

"I liked her."

"Not when we lived in New Jersey. You didn't approve when I'd offer to go shopping for Ma at the drugstore or those other places, hoping I'd run into Julie. You kept saying I had military school to think of, that I had to make good there to prove myself. You said she was pregnant and her husband was in the Army."

"I never—"

"Yes, you did," he said. "I didn't believe you. I never told you this, but I went to see her one night, and another night—" He shook his head.

He didn't seem to know his nose was bleeding.

I said, "If I walked up to the road—"

He lifted the gun. "Julie told me about her baby business. Laughed about it; laughed at me. A hick kid from Pennsylvania." He looked pensive. "The world is small now, Ida. Planes, television. There aren't any hicks anymore." His voice was growing weaker.

"No."

"I thought when we ordered the baby, twenty thousand dollars was fair exchange." He turned his head. "Don't you think that's fair exchange?"

I nodded, clenching my teeth, trying to control their chattering.

"A night with Julie—and, hey! she called me; I didn't call her—plus a kid to show for it. If it wasn't a boy, and God how we needed a boy, we'd have another go-around. All with my wife's permission. Great?" He waved the gun under my chin. "Great?"

"G-great."

"Linda wanted a baby, and she likes money as much as I do. But that wasn't how they worked, Benny said. I didn't get near Julie."

Of course not.

"You know why?" Howie's gun was still that close to my face. "Do you?"

"Arti-artificial insemination." I couldn't seem to control my chattering teeth when my mouth was open.

"Yep." He took the gun away from my face. "Me, and Benny and his little old test tube, or whatever the hell it was. The best plans—" He took a deep shuddering breath. "Then, you, with all your photographs of dear old New Jersey."

"I don't have any." Dear heaven, the blood.

"Yes, you do. Ask Julie. You have some of her when she was baking a babe for a friend of hers in Plains. That kid of yours was always sneaking around snapping people. She says Ma's sure to make a connection."

"Your—" I clenched my teeth, opened my mouth. "Your mother never knew Julie." I pulled up my legs. It was so cold. "You worried about those photos for nothing. So did Benny Quick. You should have stayed out of my garden trying to scare me, you should have stayed out of my house, you needn't have tried to burn it down. I never had those prints!"

He didn't hear me. He lifted his head. "Linda, would you get me a cup of coffee?"

"Yes," I said. "In a minute."

"I want it now. Is it nine o'clock yet?"

"Not quite."

"Remind me. Have to call Julie. Every night I call Julie. Have to know when that baby's coming. Then after, I want Julie on the first plane out of here. You're not mad at me, are you?"

"No." I remembered him at the phone in the entrance hall the night of the Brocks' party, his look of annoyance. Julie wasn't home to take his call; she'd been in the solarium with the gray-wigged Benny, telling *him* to get home. "Why should I be mad?"

"What you don't know can't hurt you, baby, and I'm never going to tell you. So you can't be mad, can you?"

"No."

"That's good. I did what you said. I didn't let them bury their garbage pails out on your mother's back property. No way, I said; no way."

"What did you do with them?"

"Some junk pit back in the mountains somewhere. I threw in Benny's suitcase and the pillow too. He didn't even notice." Howie tried to turn. "Linda, where are you?"

"Here." Oh, so cold.

"Linda, we have to sell the house to pay Julie off. It's temporary, baby, and think what we'll be getting. We'll have the only son, carry on the name. And income from that trust for the rest of our lives." Howie dropped his head to the crook of his arm. The gun was still in his hand. "Ida, tell Linda to hurry. I need some coffee right away."

"I'll tell her."

The rain wouldn't let up. It pounded down; pounded and pounded. Howie's hair, in the lights of my car, protected from the rain by the fender, was still as wavy and softly golden as it had been when he was young and only innocently wicked.

After a while I took the gun from his limp hand. I pulled myself up by a limb, climbed over a tree trunk, and scrambled up the bank to the road.

24

At home we had been waiting for rain a long time. Here, it never was going to stop.

I looked back at the huge tree across the road. A dark fortress.

When the car rounded the curve coming toward me with its blinding headlights, I lifted an arm against the glare. I whirled, darting back down into the trees.

There was the sound of brakes. Car doors slammed. Voices.

"Ida? Ida— Hey! Henderson, here—

"Come on, hon." Walt's voice. I heard him moving down toward me through the brush, slipping and sliding. The sudden spotlight made night bright as day. Walt, sideways, bracing himself against a tree, reached out a hand. I grasped it, tears crowding close. "I want to go home."

"That's where we're going."

Walt pulling me, we scrambled up the bank. Chief Henderson was waiting. "What are you doing with a gun, Ida?"

"It's Howie's." I gave it to him.

"Where is Howie?"

"Down there."

"Where?"

"Under a car and a tree." I turned. "Yes, that's where he is." I pointed. "Can't you see the lights? They're from my car, and they're still working. Howie's almost dead."

The two men exchanged glances. Turning back, I saw them. "Sounds like shock," the Chief said. "Better get to a hospital."

Another car rounded the curve, its headlights bearing down on us. It pulled to a stop behind the patrol car. A big man in uniform slid out, shoulders hunched against the rain, and joined us in the pool of light. It was Officer Barlow. He handed the car keys to Walt. "You all right, Mrs. Pelham?"

"Yes." I wiped my dripping chin with a cupped palm.

"We have a couple of blankets in the trunk," Officer Barlow said to Walt.

Walt nodded. "Yes, we could use one, thanks."

Chief Henderson was talking on the radio in the patrol car. Officer Barlow went to the trunk. I sloshed through puddles to give the Chief the two limp strips of paper from my left pocket. Still talking, his eyes on me, he took them, nodding. He knew what they were.

"Ida, come on, now—"

The car was warm. There was a gray blanket on the seat, and some wrinkled white rags. Walt helped me wrap myself in the blanket. He handed me the rags. "They'll keep your hair from dripping."

I looked around at the familiar upholstery. "Why, this is your car," I said as Walt got in the other side.

He nodded. "Barlow drove it up. I came with Henderson."

I hadn't noticed that. "I don't want to go to the hospital."

"They could dry you off, lend you some warm clothes."

The heater was on high. "I'm getting warm. I'm glad you're here."

"Me, too. When you didn't get back, I called Linda at the cabin. She said you'd left hours ago. She said Howie phoned to tell her not to go out because the driving was bad, but you were already pulling away."

"Howie didn't call about driving conditions," I said. "He wanted to know where I was; when I'd left." I looked over at him. How very dear he was. "I always think the same thing when you're late, that you've been in an accident."

"I'm pretty good about telephoning."

"Yes, and I appreciate it. Walt, I was in an accident, but it wasn't my fault."

"Why don't you tell me about it?"

I told him about it, sometimes repeating myself, pausing now and then, remembering, seeing Howie's face. Walt prompted me with quiet questions.

I pushed the button to the glove compartment, and reached in for a tissue. "I wondered how Howie was able to find Julie after all those years since New Jersey. But he said she called him; he didn't call her."

"Julie called him because he told Mrs. Tully on the phone he wanted to get in touch with her."

"Did the Chief tell you that?"

"On the way up. Howie's phone call to Mrs. Tully, when Henderson heard about it, was what made him suspect Howie. Then when he heard where you'd gone this afternoon—" He stopped. "Tully said his wife didn't know who Howie Brock was. All she remembers is that he called Julie by the name she used in Plains. Mrs. Tully passed the message along the next time she heard from Julie."

"Ellen said those two never were seen together; nobody knew they were friends."

"Ellen did, didn't she?"

We drove for a while in silence. "Howie must have taken all his money back after he killed Julie," I said. "If he didn't tell his wife about the murders, he couldn't have told her about the money, could he? Maybe it's in his car. I'm sure that's where those bank straps came from."

"Or the money's stashed away in a bank account somewhere. Henderson will find it."

We had driven out of the rain. We were back on Route 80 now. I said: "Eleanor Brock was always so sure Howie's children would be boys, if only his wife would get to it."

Greedy, greedy, greedy. Benny Quick had said that. The Brock family and its fortune, and the crown prince one of her own personal productions. How good that must have looked to Julie Gordon.

I snoozed a little, and then we were home. The temperature outside the car was the same as in, but I shivered. The grass under our feet was stiff, dry. It needed water.

We each had two cups of steaming clam broth, right out of the can, and a few oyster crackers. Then we got into the shower. That's about the time they were wheeling Howie into the Emergency Room in that little hospital in the Poconos. The same time that Linda and her mother-in-law, sitting together outside the Emergency Room door, came as close to being friends as they'll ever be. For a few hours.

Howie died at ten to six in the morning. Eleanor Brock telephoned from the hospital. She was calm; just said she wanted us to know before we heard it on the morning news. And if we knew where her husband was—

We didn't.

According to the media, the conjecture is that Howie killed two people with the same gun he had pointed at me because he was being blackmailed. It was known that young Brock was a heavy gambler, and deeply in debt.

If Eleanor Brock suspects the real story, she'll never tell. Neither will Pearl.

And, as Chief Henderson says, Linda, ensconced in her apartment with the beautiful baby boy Brock, sure as hell won't.

They have only the bits and pieces, those three women.

Anyway, what does it matter now?

Our garden is in terrible trouble. I use the sprinklers when we're not advised against it.

Here, it's still hot.

Here, we're still waiting for rain.